FIRST EDITION 2018

Book design by Megyn Ward

Cover design by Megyn Ward

Cover photos by Adobe stock

Also by Megyn Ward

The Gilroy Clan

Pushing Patrick
Claiming Cari
Having Henley
Conquering Conner
(Coming April, 2018!)
Destroying Declan
(Coming October, 2018!)
Taming Tesla
(Coming December, 2018!)

The Kings of Brighton

Tobias
Grayson
(coming January, 2019!)

One Night

Drive
Grind

With Shanen Black

Paradise Lost

Diving Deep
Hard Dive
Tidal Wave

ONE

Claire
2013

"Seven... eight... nine... ten—ready or not, here I come!" I shout before uncovering my eyes and turning around. The living room is deceptively quiet, considering I happen to babysit for the most rambunctious five-year-old on the planet. "Where could Simon be?" I say it loud, waiting for the answering, telltale giggle that usually answers the question.

No giggle.

I creep around the couch and check behind it before going for his favorite spot. Whipping the living room curtains aside, I stir up a flurry of dust bunnies but no Simon.

"Hmmm…" I call out, heading for the tiny dining room off the kitchen. "I wonder if he has invisible superpowers?" There's the giggle. Under the dining room table.

I tip-toe around the table, suppressing a laugh when I see that the king-sized bed sheet we used to build a pillow fort is hopelessly askew and showing Simon perfectly. He's sitting under the table with his eyes squeezed shut in an *if-I-can't-see-her-she-can't-see-me* sort of way. Hunkering down, I boop him on the nose with my finger. "I see you."

As soon as I touch the tip of my nose to his finger, Simon dissolves into a fit of giggles. "You found me," he says, his eyes popping open.

"You're my best friend," I tell him, ruffling his mop of dark brown hair. "I'll always find you... ready to help me start dinner?"

It's not really my job. Simon's older brother should've been home an hour ago, but he sent me a text saying, *Got caught up. Can you start dinner?* Makings for spaghetti are sitting out on the counter and Simon's on a pretty tight schedule.

I might as well make myself useful.

Right. You just want to help. It has nothing to do with the fact that Simon's brother is so scorching hot that you'd probably do just about anything he asked you to do.

Simon nods, crawling out from under the table before taking me by the hand to lead me into the kitchen. Boosting him up to the sink, I help him wash his hands before setting him at the table in his booster seat. "Ready to squish?" Ignoring the jar of store-bought sauce on the counter, I scrounge up a few cans of stewed tomatoes. Opening them, I pour them into a large bowl.

Simon wiggles his fingers at me. "Ready Freddy."

I set the bowl in front of him, and he digs in, using his small, chubby fingers to break up the tomatoes for the sauce. Every time he pops a tomato in his fist, he cackles like a maniac.

Damn, I love this kid.

I put a pot of water on to boil before chopping garlic and onions, adding them to the pan with a drizzle of olive oil and some dried basil I found in the spice cabinet. Digging around for oregano, my phone starts to ring.

"Jax!" Simon calls out, automatically assuming it's his older brother calling me. Just hearing his name makes my stomach flip, leaving me nauseous and giddy, all at the same time. I pick up my phone, hoping the kid is right, even though all he ever says to me when he calls is, *hey, can you pick Simon from daycare* or *hey, do you know how to make meatloaf?* or *can you sit for Simon on Tuesday?*

Which are stupid questions.

Of course, I'll pick Simon up and of course, I know how to make meatloaf.

I've been head chef at Chez St. James for seven years now. Since my mother packed her bags and left us when I was eleven. And spending time with Simon is one of my all-time favorite things to do. I'd even offer to do it for free if I didn't think my willingness to hang out with her five-year-old for free would make his mom question my mental health.

Still, a girl can hope that someday, the boy she's marginally obsessed with will call her one day and say *hey, do you want to go out sometime?*

But it's not Jaxon calling. It's my sister, Brianna. My twin sister. We aren't identical—as a matter of fact, if you didn't know better, you'd swear we aren't even related.

"Not Jax," I say, flashing Simon the phone. She babysat for him once while I had the flu a few years ago. It didn't go well. As soon as he sees my sister's duck-lip selfie on the screen, he curls his lip up at my phone and pops a tomato in his fist.

Did I mention how much I love this kid?

Laughing, I answer the phone, putting it on speaker before propping it up on the counter. "What's up?" I say, running my knife through a bell pepper I found wilting in the crisper.

"When are you coming home?" Bri says over the din of what sounds like a live deejay. We just graduated high school, and our father is out of town, so it's an actual possibility.

"Are you having a party?" I toss the bell pepper into the pan before adding a pinch of salt to the pot of water simmering to a boil on the back of the stove.

"Party is a strong word—" In the background, someone shouts the *keg is here!* "—it's just a few friends... so, when are you coming home?"

"I'm not sure." To be honest, I'm not even sure I want to come home. Staying here and playing hide-and-seek with Simon is more my speed. Still, I look at the clock. It's after six now. I should've been home an hour ago. "Mrs. Bennett doesn't get off until eleven and Jaxon gets off—"

The backdoor opens behind me, and I feel my stomach do its tilt-a-whirl thing again because it's him. It's Jaxon, and even though I see him almost every day, I still get a little bit lightheaded when I do.

"Jaxon gets off when you finally open that bank vault you call a vagina and—"

Oh, my god.

It all happens at once. Jaxon walking through the door and Simon's excited shout, all while Bri's voice rings out loud and clear, the phone's volume up high enough that it sounds like she's standing in the kitchen with me. There's no way he didn't just hear what she said.

I drop the knife in my hand and it clatters to the floor while I jab my finger at the screen, knocking the phone over. I don't succeed in turning off the speakerphone, but I do succeed in hanging up on my sister all together. Which is even better. If I could load her and her big mouth into a cannon and shoot her across Lake Michigan, I would.

Back still turned, I listen to Simon, yammering at his brother a mile-a-minute while I beg the floor to open up and swallow me whole.

I have a major thing for Jaxon Bennett. Have *had* a major thing for him since he and his family moved here when Simon was a baby. I was thirteen and Jaxon was fifteen. Five years is a long time to want something you know you're never going to get. It was bad enough, suffering in silence. Now that he knows, I might have to fake my own death and join the French Foreign Legion.

My phone keeps ringing. I answer it because *not* answering feels like some sort of acknowledgment of what my sister just broadcasted. "What?" I mutter, while behind me, I hear the scrape of Simon's kitchen chair and Jaxon telling him to go wash his hands.

"Was I on speaker phone?" It sounds like she's moved to a more quiet part of the house. "Oh my god, is he *there*?"

"Yes and yes." I turn the heat down on the veggies I have going in the pan. "What do you want?"

"Ice," she says in a small voice. Bri isn't the most sensitive person that ever lived, but she's always been careful with my feelings. Benefit of being her twin, I guess. "I just wanted you to swing by the store on your way home and grab a couple bags of ice... Claire, I'm—"

"Ice. Got it." Breath catches in my throat when I feel Jaxon move behind me, getting closer. The bowl of pulverized tomatoes appears in front of me. "Jaxon's back so I'll be home in a bit." I hang up the phone, tossing it on the counter, in favor of the bowl of tomatoes he put in front of me. "Thanks," I say, shooting him a brief smile that I hope like hell says, *my sister is an idiot. Actually, I think she might be on drugs*. I pour the bowl into the skillet in front of me and give it a good stir before lowering the heat to let the sauce thicken.

He's still standing next to me, hip leaned against the counter, head lowered just a bit so he can see my face. He's huge. At well over six-feet, he towers over me. Broad shoulders and chest. Thick, powerful arms. Long, muscular legs. Huge hands. There's a lot about Jaxon Bennett that gets me hot and bothered but for some reason, thinking about his hands sends a flush of heat rushing over me, from head to toe. God, he smells good. Like sawdust and watermelon. Why does he always smell like watermelon?

"You know..." He turns, bracing his back against the counter beside me so that we're facing each other. "When I asked if you could start dinner, I didn't mean for you to go all Martha Stewart on me." He reaches across me and drags the jar of store-bought sauce across the counter until it's sitting in front of me.

We're pretending my sister didn't announce to the entire planet that I want to tear your clothes off?

Okay. Good.

Looking up, I focus on one thing. One feature of his face because that's the only way I can be present in this conversation. I know from experience that I can't be this close to him and *not* hyperventilate without some sort of distraction.

Gaze settled on the bridge of his nose, I shake my head, making a disgusted noise in the back of my throat. "*Pssft*." I look down at the jar, reaching out to push it back. "That stuff tastes like wallpaper paste. I have no idea what wallpaper tastes like— it's just something my grand—"

The second our hands connect, I stop talking. Stop breathing. His fingers slide over the back of my hand, leaving a trail of fire in their wake.

I watch as his broad, callused hand, very deliberately, turns mine in its grip. "What would we do without you, Claire?" he says in a low tone while the pad of his thumb sweeps over the underside of my wrist. Slow, soft circles that shoot up my arm and down my spine. Lower and deeper until I can feel each stroke of his thumb against every place I want him to touch me.

Oh.

I guess we're not *pretending...*

I look up at him. The whole Jaxon. Deep brown eyes. Dark hair. Strong jaw. Full mouth. Slightly crooked nose that looks like it's been broken once or twice, which instead of messing up the aesthetic, makes him even hotter for some reason.

He's looking down at me, his gaze dark and unreadable and I get the feeling he's thinking about kissing me, which is crazy.

Guys like Jaxon don't kiss me.

Correction: *guys* don't kiss me.

Period.

Guys kiss Bri. Want Bri. They don't want me. Plain Jane, jeans and sneakers me. They just don't.

The most I ever get is a random, *I've never fucked twins before* like that's enough to get me all hot and bothered. Like I should be eager to give my virginity to some guy who's just looking to check *nailed twins* off his pre-college checklist.

No thanks.

He's leaning into me, his lips hovering, inches above mine, slightly open. "Claire..." My name sounds rough, uneven, his gaze nailed to my mouth.

Ohmygod, he is *going to kiss me.*

Don'tpassout

Don'tpassout

Don'tpas—

"I'm hungry," Simon announces from the doorway, and I jerk my wrist out of his grip like we were caught doing something wrong. Which we weren't. I'm eighteen. Old enough to be kissed. More than kissed. The fact that I haven't been eats at me, almost shames me, even though I know the reason why. The reason why is standing right in front of me. I don't want to be kissed—*more than kissed*—by just anyone.

I want to be more than kissed by Jaxon Bennett.

"Eight minutes," I say, reaching for the box of pasta. My hands are shaking, and I fumble with the top for a second before I finally just rip it off. I drop dried noodles into boiling water before adding another generous pinch of salt.

I step back from the stove while wiping my hands on a dish towel. Jaxon is still looking at me. Watching me. "I've got to get home." I'm not sure which brother I'm saying it to, but as soon as I do, Simon lets out a wail of protest that snags at my heart.

"I'll be back—"

"Simon, should we ask Claire to stay?" Jaxon says, still looking at me.

"Yeah!" Simon runs at me, throwing his arms around my legs, digging his chin into my belly so he can look up at me. "Stay for dinner, *plleease.*"

I drop a hand on his head, running my fingers through his dark hair—the same, exact shade as his older brother's—looking down into his pleading face.

Did I happen to mention how much I love this kid?

I sigh, my resolve to get myself out of here and away from Jaxon before I do or say something stupid, wobbling under the weight of his stare.

"Okay," I say. "I'll stay."

TWO

Jaxon
2018

My hands tighten around the bar, and I lift my knees, jacking them up to my chest while pushing out and up with my arms. The bar explodes from its slot to land in the one above it.

I do it again.

And again.

Again.

Again.

Until I'm at the top of the salmon ladder, hanging ten feet in the air. I can feel the scar slashed across my lower abdomen. The still-mending muscle underneath it starts to pull under my considerable weight.

I ignore it.

If my surgeon knew what I was doing, she'd shit a brick, but whatever. It's been 3 months. I'm tired of sitting around. To be honest, I got tired of sitting around two and a half months ago.

What she doesn't know won't hurt her.

I've got goals, and they don't include letting myself go soft.

"Phone," Simon says behind me. I had no idea he was standing there. If I had, I probably wouldn't have pushed it so hard. He's a worrier, like my mom.

Giving the ladder a final lunge, I unseat the bar, taking it with me as I make the ten-foot drop. I'm 6'7, so it's not nearly as impressive as it sounds. Slamming the bar back into the bottom rung, I turn to find Simon watching me.

He's a quiet kid, and it's been awkward between us since I got back. Five years ago, he was five-years-old and my little shadow. Everywhere I went, he wanted to be. If he wasn't sleeping or eating, he was perched on my shoulders. Sometimes even when he *was* eating or sleeping. Now he looks at me like I'm a total stranger.

Which I guess I am.

Scrubbing at my sweaty chest with a towel, I cross the space between us, fixing an easy smile on my face. "Thanks, kid." I take the phone from him and reach out with my other hand to ruffle his hair the way I used to. He ducks out the door before I get the chance.

Guess he's still mad at me.

Letting my free hand drop, I lift the phone to my ear. "Bennett." I bark it, tossing the sweaty towel into the washing machine shoved into the corner of the detached garage. With the weight bench, salmon ladder, and punching bag it's more gym than laundry room. I keep my ride off-site. Parking in Chicago costs a fucking fortune, but it's worth it for the added security.

"Hey—got a job for you." It's Joe. He thinks salutations are a waste of time. When it comes to him, I agree. "Guy needs a driver, last minute."

"For?" Last minute jobs are usually shit— which is a coincidence because so are my Saturday nights. Off weekends usually consist of me trying to awkwardly connect with Simon until he gets tired of me pestering him and disappears into his room for the rest of the night. Then I usually end up back out here, seeing how far I can push myself before my scar busts open.

Good times.

"Bachelorette party." I hear his desk chair creak as he leans back to prop his feet on his desk.

Bachelorette party?

Yup. Total and complete shit.

"No way," I say shaking my head. I'd rather bleed out on the mats than spend a Saturday night wrangling drunk chicks and mopping puke out of the back of my ride. "You know that's not my thing. Get Mullens or Graham to do it."

"Come on, man." He starts to wheedle, using a tone that instantly sets my teeth on edge. "The ladies love you."

Yeah. They love me. Because I'm under thirty and actually give a shit about keeping myself in fighting shape. Regardless, I don't work out and stay sharp because I enjoy getting groped by drunk bridesmaids.

Instead of arguing I repeat myself. "Get Mullens or Graham to do it." I'm freelance, not a regular employee. That means I can pick and choose my assignments. I don't have to take his shit jobs, and he knows it.

"Can't." Josephson blows out a sigh. "Got both of 'em working."

I don't say anything. He wants me on this, he's gonna have to work for it.

"Come on." He says it like he's coaxing a shy virgin out of her panties. "I gotta have you on this one—you know you're my guy."

"Don't stroke me, man," I laugh. "It doesn't feel half as good as you think it does."

"Look—I'll pay you rate and a quarter." I hear his chair squeak again. He's sitting up straight again. Ready to get down to business. "How's that sound?"

Desperate, that's how it sounds. "Double." Unlike the other clowns he has driving for him, I have my own ride—a 2017 black Chrysler stretch. I don't need him. If I had the time to build a clientele, I'd tell this fucker to jump in the Chicago River. And he knows it.

"Fuck—you're pretty but not *that* pretty, Bennett." He laughs. "I can drive it myself."

Joe looks like Danny DeVito, only half as tall and twice as ugly. "Have fun, princess. Remember, the gas pedal is on the right." I hang up and toss the phone on top of the dryer so I can start a load of towels. It starts rattling and buzzing before I even have a chance to add the soap.

"Bennett."

"Rate and a half."

I hang up. Measure out some laundry soap and pour it into the machine. The phone starts its rattle and buzz routine again.

"Bennet."

"Double," he huffs into the phone. "Guy requested you special. I can't put anyone else on it."

His admission piques my interest almost as much as it pisses me off. I get a bonus if I'm requested by name. A bonus he had no intention of giving me. I put that away for later. "What guy? I thought you said it was a bachelorette."

"I dunno—some rich fucker out in the burbs. It's his daughter getting married. Reservation came through online—some doctor type's credit card paid the bill in full. That's all I know." He's getting antsy. "You takin' the double or what?"

"No—but I'll take triple." I don't like being fucked with, and I hate being lied to. "*And* my bonus."

Silence. Probably running the math in his head. When he comes to the same conclusion I did—that not only is he going to make a goddamned dime off me, but that my bonus is going to come out of his ass— he sighs. "Fine, asshole," he breathes into the phone. "Triple."

"And?" I slam the lid and spin the dial.

He curses under his breath. "And your bonus."

"Pleasure doing business with you, Joe." I cut the call and toss the phone before he can start bitching.

THREE

Claire

He looks like Lurch." Bri looks at me over her shoulder from her post at the window. "You know, like from *The Addam's Family*?"

"That's not very nice," I say, scowling up at her as I bend over to wedge on my heels. Standing up straight, I tug at the hem of my skirt, feeling a little self-conscious about its length. Bri insisted on matching dresses, which means I feel like a hooker.

"I know." She gives me a shrug, totally nonplussed. "Doesn't make me wrong though."

Curious, I move to stand next to her at the window, and she scoots over so I can check out the driver my father hired for the evening. It's Bri's bachelorette party and we're heading into the city. Dinner. Dancing. Public. Crowds.

Just the thought freaks me out.

It's been ages since I've been... anywhere, really. I've been pretty much stuck here at home with my dad since I graduated high school. Seriously, the biggest thing I did when I turned eighteen was get my pharmacy tech license. I'm twenty-two, and I've never been to a nightclub. Never bought a drink at a bar. The most I've done is buy a bottle of wine at the grocery store.

So, yeah. Life so far has been pretty awesome.

Looking out the window, I aim my gaze at the man standing in our driveway, next to the sleek black limousine our father hired for the night. He's tall, I'll give Bri that much. Impossibly tall—at least 6'5—but that's where the similarities end. This guy is massive. Even beneath the somber suit, I can tell he's built. His muscles have muscles. His dark hair is clipped short. He stands with his feet shoulder-width apart, his hands clasped behind his back, face aimed forward.

"You need your head examined," I tell my sister, looking down at the circular driveway. "He's a little stiff, but he doesn't look anything like—"

He looks up. Not like he's searching for something. Like knows I'm here. Exactly where I am. Knows I'm checking him out and wants me to know I'm caught. He's wearing sunglasses to block out the late afternoon sun, but that doesn't matter. I feel our eyes connect and my stomach does a slow roll before taking the express route to my feet. Even from behind his dark lenses, I feel the intensity of those deep brown eyes skewer me. Pin me in place. No one else has ever given me that tilt-a-whirl feeling.

Not ever.

Holy shit.

I step back, away from the window, stumbling a bit in my heels.

"Jesus, Claire." Bri looks at me. "Are you okay?" She takes my place at the window and peers through it. "You look like—"

"I'm fine," I tell her, shaking my head. "I..." Pressing my hand to my stomach, I take a deep breath. Let it out slowly. "I forgot a sweater." I turn, heading for the door. We're in Bri's old bedroom. She lives in the city with her fiancé but has been staying here, intent on no sex until the wedding night. It's been a very long, very crabby two-weeks.

"A sweater?" Now she's looking at me like I'm nuts. "It's August."

I nod, agreeing with her, even as I'm stepping out into the hall. Ducking into the nearest room with an open door. The guest bathroom. I shut the door behind me and lean against it. Eyes squeezed shut, I try to get my breathing under control.

Calm down, Claire.

Flipping on the light, I push myself away from the door. Making my way over to the sink, I aim my gaze at the mirror above it. My cheeks are flushed. Eyes a little glassy. My skin is hot. I look and feel like I have a fever.

It's not a fever.

It's him.

Jaxon Bennett is here.

Here.

At my house.

"Claire." Bri bangs on the bathroom door. "We need to leave now if we're going to pick everyone up *and* make our dinner reservation."

For a brief moment, I consider telling her I'm sick. To go without me. *Have a good time. See you in the morning. Pictures or it didn't happen.*

But I can't do that. I'm her maid of honor. I'm also her babysitter. Bri has every intention of getting sloppy tonight, and it's my job to make sure she makes it through the night with as much of her dignity intact as humanly possible.

"Okay," I call through the door before taking another deep breath. "I'll be out in a minute."

I hear her sigh. "Hurry up," she says before I hear the sound of her heels clicking down the hall.

Staring at myself in the mirror, I give my reflection a stern lecture. *Jaxon's not here to take you on a date, for Christ's sake. He's a limo driver. A very expensive designated driver.*

He's just a guy.

But he isn't just a guy.

He's *the* guy.

The guy who's firmly planted himself between me and every other guy I've ever dated.

The guy I've been half in love with since I was fifteen years old.

The guy I gave my virginity to when I was eighteen.

The guy who disappeared the morning after, without a trace.

FOUR

Jaxon

2013

I can tell you the exact moment I started looking at Claire St. James as more than just Simon's babysitter.

She was sixteen, almost seventeen. Still in high school. I was eighteen and just graduated. Working construction, same as now, and taking night classes at community college. My mom works second shift at a nursing home so when Claire agreed to watch Simon so I could make my classes, it was a godsend.

Anyway, she'd been watching Simon for a while, long enough for us to get ourselves into a comfortable routine. Usually, when I come home, she's at the kitchen table doing homework, and Simon's in bed, upstairs. We'd make small talk while she gathered her stuff, and then I stand at the back door and watch to make sure that she got in her car safely. Gailena, Illinois: population 3,317 isn't exactly a hotbed of crime and corruption but knowing she's safe makes me feel better.

This particular night, when I came home, her homework was spread out all over the kitchen table like always, but she was nowhere to be seen.

I don't know what I thought—just that she was supposed to be there but *wasn't*. I called her name. Nothing.

I charged up the stairs, and headed for the bedroom I share with Simon, and there they were. Simon in his little toddler-sized bed and Claire in mine.

Seeing her in my bed did something to me. Made me see things differently. *Her* differently. Woke a part of me I'd shut down a long time ago. In an instant, everything changed.

Standing there in the doorway, looking at her, I had the urge to go to her. Pull her clothes off and put my mouth and hands all over every part of her that was soft and pink that I could reach.

And then she woke up. Apologized for sleeping in my bed. Told me that Simon had a nightmare and wanted her to stay with him. I told her it was fine. I broke routine. Told her I was going to jump in the shower instead of walking her out because I suddenly didn't trust myself around her. I'm not sure how long I stayed in the bathroom. It felt like hours. When I finally emerged, she was gone.

I've always thought she was pretty, even before things got weird on my end. Light brown hair. Wide eyes, their color caught somewhere between blue and green. Full breasts. Soft curves. The kind of mouth guys dream about. The kind that was made for—

The point is, it's been brewing for a while. At least it has been for me. Two years later and I still can't breathe around her, get within two feet of her, without having to fight the urge to get her under me. I can't even lay in my own bed without thinking about what I'd do to her if she were laying in it with me.

I've always managed it though because I never once felt like the feelings were mutual. She's always kept her distance. Been polite. Accommodating. Simon adores her, and clearly, the feeling is mutual. Bottom line: without her, my mom and I would be screwed. I never felt like I could afford to mess that up. My family needed her too much.

But that was before.

Before I heard what her sister said. Saw the panicked flush erupt across the back of her neck. The way she responded when I touched that back of her hand. Her wrist. The way her breath caught in her throat. Eyes glazed over. Lips parted.

Before any of that happened, I was prepared to live with the random fantasies and raging hard-ons. The cold showers and mandatory masturbation sessions that having her around induced.

Now?

No. Not so much.

Now, I'm wondering how many times I can make her come between putting Simon to bed and my mom pulling into the driveway while I pull bath duty, and she cleans up the dinner mess downstairs.

The weird part of it all is that when I think about her, it's not always about fucking her. Most of the time, I just think about her. I *like* her. I like that she turns her nose up at jarred spaghetti sauce. That she plays hide-and-seek and builds blanket forts with

Simon. That she's sarcastic and sweet and way smarter than I'll ever be.

I like her.

I might even love her a little bit.

"Jax?" Simon calls out to me from the bathroom.

Shit. "What's up, buddy?"

He's five now and thinks he's entirely too old for supervised baths. The compromise is that if I *have* to supervise, I do it from the hallway, outside the open bathroom door.

"I like Claire."

Double shit.

"Yeah..." I sigh because I know where this is coming from. What he's thinking about. "I like her too."

"I'm glad she stayed for dinner."

"Me too."

I hear him pull the plug on the tub. Water getting sucked down the drain in a fast swirl. A few seconds later, he's standing in the doorway, wrapped in his favorite Scooby Doo towel. "Do we have to leave?"

The question stings. Before Simon was born, we moved around a lot. Floated from town to town. State to state. By the time I was his age, we'd covered most of the midwest. I'd have to look at my own birth certificate to be able to tell you where I was even born. I don't know what it's like to put down roots. Or at least I didn't. Not until Simon was born. We've lived here for nearly five years now and I thought leaving was going to be easy. It was always the plan. Not one my mom was crazy about, but she understood that college wasn't in the cards for me. That I don't have time to waste in a four-year university, trying to find my way in life like the people I went to high school with.

It's why I pretty much keep to myself. A few acquaintances but no real friends. No real relationships. No girls. I secluded myself in preparation for what's coming. I never thought in a million years that my plans would be in danger of being derailed by someone as sweet and as simple as Claire St. James.

I was wrong.

"Yeah, buddy—we do." I reach down and pick him up, carrying him down the hall to our room. I put him down and give him a good rub down with the towel before handing him his pajamas. He puts them on while I hang up his towel. When I come back, he's already in bed. "Simon burrito?" I ask even though Claire is waiting for me downstairs because it's our thing and nothing's more important to me than Simon.

He scowls and nods. "Can we take her with us?"

I like the idea. I like it entirely too much. I let myself think about it for a second. Telling her how I feel. What I want. Ask her to be with me.

Us.

It would never work. There are things about me I can never tell her. Things that would make her run, fast and far, away from me. I'd rather leave her behind than take the risk of having her look at me like I was some sort of freak.

"Fraid not," I say, tucking his blankets around him as tight as I can get them. "Claire's got a family that needs her."

His chin wobbles for a moment before he sets it into a firm frown. "But I need her too." He glares at me, tears in his eyes, like this is all my fault. Like I'm the reason we have to leave. "I don't want to leave."

Neither do I, buddy. Neither do I.

FIVE

Claire

I've never cleaned a kitchen so slowly in my life.

I make a plate for Jaxon's mom and cover it with foil before putting it in the oven—something I've done for my own father a million times. He's a cardiologist and makes the sixty-mile commute to and from Chicago every day. With Bri either out with friends or at cheer practice, there weren't a lot of family dinners for us growing up. It was mostly me, eating alone in my room, in front of an old movie.

Moving on, I start the dishes, listening to the sounds of Simon's bath—the excited squeak of his voice. The low, answering murmur of Jaxon's. They're arguing because Simon thinks he's entirely too old for supervised baths. Jaxon compromises by sitting in the hallway outside the door.

There are dishes from this morning, plus what Simon and I used throughout the day. I do those too. Since they don't have a dishwasher, I wash them by hand, moving slowly. Trying to draw this out as long as I can. Once the kitchen is cleaned, and everything is put away, I won't have an excuse to stay.

When I agreed to stay, I texted Bri, telling her she would have to find someone else to make an ice run, that I'd been invited to stay for dinner. Her answering text was an entire screen filled with eggplant emojis.

"I didn't ask you to stay for dinner so you could do the dishes," Jaxon says behind me. I didn't even hear him come downstairs. Something as big as Jaxon Bennett should not be allowed to move so quietly.

"Technically, *you* didn't ask me to stay for dinner," I say while running a newly washed plate under the stream of hot water from the tap. "Simon did."

He doesn't answer me. Instead, I feel his hands slide around my waist, turning me toward him. "You would've said no if I'd asked," he tells me. Lifting me like I weigh next to nothing, he sets me down on the counter next to the sink. "To get what I want, I'll take my help where I can get it." He takes the dishcloth out of my hand and steps in front of the sink. "Was your sister mad when you told her you were staying?"

I think about the screen full of eggplant emojis she sent me and nearly tip over into the sink. "No. She knows that parties aren't my thing—if I weren't here, I'd be in my room, hiding."

He gives me a smile. *The* smile. The one that says he understands exactly what I'm saying. "What is your thing?" He runs a glass under the tap and sets it in the drainer.

I shrug. "I don't really have a *thing*— unless you count hanging out with Simon."

"Hanging out? You say it like it's fun or something." He looks at me, still towering over me even though I'm sitting on the counter.

"It *is* fun," I say, tilting my head a little. "I like Simon."

He shuts off the water and stares at the sink for a moment before he looks at me. "Is that the only reason you're here? To hang out with Simon?"

I feel a flush sweep across the back of my neck. "I like Simon," I say, repeating myself like a dummy. "I like your mom and—"

"You like me." He has a strange way of asking questions that aren't really questions.

I nod. Take a deep breath and let it out slowly. There's no use in denying it or playing dumb. He heard Bri on the phone earlier. I know he did. Better just to admit it and move on. "But my feelings for you have nothing to do with the way I feel about Simon. I'd still be—"

Before I can finish my sentence, Jaxon moves. Slipping into the space between my legs, his hands slide lower, gripping my hips to pull me even closer until I can feel the press of him widen the juncture of my thighs. "You have feelings." His face is inches from mine, his mouth hovering so close I can smell the minty tinge of toothpaste.

I nod. "You brushed your teeth." I don't know why but knowing that tips me over the edge. Suddenly, my heart is going crazy, flopping and twisting in my chest. Knocking the breath out of my lungs every time it beats.

The corner of his mouth kicks up in a crooked smile. "I believe in being prepared for all possible contingencies."

"What contingency is this?" I'm not sure how I'm still conscious, let alone speaking in complete sentences.

His fingers dig into my hips, the press of them hard, almost urgent, at total odds with the easy-going smile on his face. "The *I've been thinking about kissing you all night* contingency."

"Oh..." I breathe the word, and it comes out shaky. Sounds far away. "Is it because of what Bri said?" Not that I care. He could be kissing me in order to save the world from imminent destruction, and I would've been on board with it. Anything that gets his mouth on mine gets a thumbs up in my book.

"No." He leans in, and my eyes slip closed, just before I feel the press of his lips against the line of my jaw. "I pretty much think about kissing you all the time."

"You do?" Is this a dream? Am I sleeping? If I am, don't wake me up. Ever.

"Uh huh." His mouth moves along the curve of my jaw before moving on to my throat. "Ever since the night I found you sleeping in my bed." His teeth nip against the tendons in my neck. "Now I can't even lie down in it without thinking about what it would be like to fuck you," he whispers in my ear before taking my lobe between his teeth.

Ohmygod.

"I like old movies," I say softly as a shiver shoots through me, racking my body from head to toe.

"Movies?" I feel his mouth curve into a smile against the soft spot behind my ear while the hand on my hip moves upward, slipping under the hem of my T-shirt. "Are we talking about the same thing?"

"You asked me what I was into..." The last word is pushed out on a shuddering breath as I feel his fingers skim along my ribcage. "Movies. I like movies."

"*Mmm…*" His voice hums along my skin, a low-level electrical current that buzzes across my skin, leaves me rattled. "I did ask that, didn't I?" he says, his fingertips following the curve of my breast.

"Yes..." My nipple hardens beneath his touch, straining against the cup of my bra. I push myself into his hand, loving the way my breast fits perfectly into his palm, the heat of it making the tip of it tingle.

The hand still on my hip digs in, pulling me closer. "I like hearing you say that." His hand slips around to cradle my ass, tucking me against him. He flexes his hips, grazing my throbbing center with the rigid length of his cock. "Say it again."

"*Oh...*" My hands, planted on the counter to keep myself steady, come up to fist themselves in his T-shirt. My knees tighten against his hips, heels digging into his ass. "*Yes.*" I have no idea what I'm saying yes to, and I don't care. All I know is that I don't want this to end. I need him to keep touching me.

He groans against my neck, his hard cock rocking against the center seam of my jeans, grinding it against my pussy while he jerks the cup of my bra down, freeing my breast.

"Jaxon..." I whimper his name softly, tipping my head back while his mouth works its way back to mine, his hips still working and flexing between my legs, each stroke of his cock pressing deeper. Pushing me closer. I can feel the pressure building. My core melting, the heat of it spreading like wildfire. I'm about to come. Just like this, with nothing but the promise of him between my legs and his mouth on my neck. I'd be embarrassed if I wasn't so far gone. "Jaxon, I'm—"

I hear a car door slam, followed by the chirp of a car alarm. Footsteps crunching across their gravel drive. The rhythm of his hips falters at the sounds.

"Shit." Jaxon lifts his head, eyes narrowing on my face before bouncing up to look at the clock above the sink. "She's early." The hand under my shirt fixes my bra, moving it back into place before slipping out to resettle on my hip.

His mom.

"Oh, god..." The thought is like a bucket of cold water dumped over my head, freezing me in place even as my face goes up in flames. She trusted me to watch Simon and here I am, practically fucking his older brother on her kitchen counter. "I shouldn't have—"

"Stop," he says, shaking his head. "You didn't do anything wrong." He leans into me, even as I hear his mom's footsteps on the front porch. "Neither of us did." He kisses me on the mouth, a soft, lingering press of lips that instantly start to pull me under. "We're both adults, remember?" He pulls back again, looking me right in the eye. "Okay?"

For a second, I'm not sure which one of us he's trying to convince. Finally, I nod my head. "Yes."

He makes a noise in the back of his throat, half groan, half growl, the hands on my hips tightening before pulling me off the counter and setting me on my feet. "You should leave."

"Now?" Usually, if I'm still here when his mom gets home, I stick around long enough to fill her in on Simon's day.

"Now. Before I stop caring about what she walks in on," Jaxon says, turning me toward the back door, just as the rattle of keys signal the opening of the front.

Before my sneakers hit the top step of the stoop, Jaxon snags me by my arm and stops me, turns me toward him. Pulls me against him. He kisses me, his mouth hitting mine with the force of a punch, his tongue sweeping in to tangle with mine, so hot and urgent that I moan, the hum of it buzzing against my lips.

With a groan, he tears himself away from me. "Your dad's out of town."

It's another non-question question. I nod, my heart in my throat. I hear his mother in the foyer, dropping her keys into the basket. Going through the mail.

He doesn't say anything else, he just lets me go. He doesn't ask if he can come over. He doesn't say he'll call or text.

Seconds later, I'm sitting in my car, across the street, trying to get my keys in the ignition. My whole body is on fire. Throbbing. I look up and out the passenger-side window.

Jaxon is standing on the back stoop, arms folded across his massive chest. He's watching to make sure I get my car started. That I'm safe. Seeing him standing there, same as always, makes me wonder if I imagined it all.

SIX

Jaxon
2018

Memories are funny things.

Five years ago, if someone asked me what Claire St. James' address was, I could've rattled it off in my sleep. Even now, I know it. I know it as well as I know my own name. I couldn't forget it if I tried.

I can't tell you how many times I've thought about her over the years. There were times when the memory of her face was the only thing that sustained me.

Kept me together. Kept me sane.

Even now, back in the world, I spend more nights than I should, remembering how she felt against me. Beneath me. Wrapped around me.

I've been with women—before Claire and after—but none of them have been her.

None of them have come close to even the memory of her. So, eventually, I stopped trying to replace her and just concentrated on trying to survive her.

I'm not sure what that makes me. I know it's not exactly healthy, the fact that I can't seem to let her go—which is fucking sad considering I did this to myself. I ruined it. I'm the one who took what she so innocently offered and then just walked away.

When I think about showing up on her doorstep, I know exactly what I'd say. I'd tell her why I left. That leaving her was the last thing I wanted to do. Make her understand that I didn't have a choice.

Which brings me back to the memory thing and why they're funny.

Even though I know the address, Even though I've worked up the fantasy of hopping on my bike and coming for her, like something out of a goddamned fairytale—a thousand different times in a thousand different ways—I don't recognize it for what it is until I'm popping open the driver's' side door and stepping onto her driveway.

That's when it hits me.

Claire St. James.

I'm here. Standing in her driveway.

And it feels like fate.

I've been home for almost six months, and I'm three months post-op. I've had plenty of time to make it happen. Make it right. But I haven't. Always find a reason to wait. I pretend that it's what's best for Simon. That we need time. That he and I need to get used to the way things are now, not how we wish they still were.

Truth is, I'm chickenshit.

Pure and simple.

Even though I've thought about making the drive, forcing the conversation—forcing her to listen to me—I never found the nerve because I was sure she would slam the door in my face. Possibly laugh in it. No way she waited for my sorry ass.

That's when I remember why I'm here.

A bachelorette party.

Jesus Christ, she's getting married.

You dumb, gutless motherfucker.

You waited too long, and now you've lost her for good. And not just you—Simon. What about Simon?

He loved her. Still talks about her. I know that the loss of her is something he blames me for. I can still see him at five-years-old, peering up at me through narrowed eyes, angry and not understanding the why of how things had to be. For him, it was simple.

Why can't we take her with us?

When am I going to stop fucking things up?

Someone is looking at me. Watching me from the second-floor window directly above my head. Has been for a while now. I can feel the trace of their gaze along my frame like it's a real, tangible thing and my skin starts to prickle under the weight of it. I feel naked. Exposed.

Stow your shit, Bennett. You're standing in an upper-class driveway in Gailena, Illinois: population 3,317—not some dirty, middle-eastern stan, *waiting to get your head blown off.*

I allow myself to look up, aiming a hard stare at the person watching me from above. I can't see who it is, but I know. The moment our eyes connect through the glass, I feel like someone's hooked jumper cables to my earlobes. It's her.

Claire.

As soon as I feel her, she's gone, the connection broken as instantly as it'd taken root, leaving me with a feeling of a momentary free fall before I slam back into my body.

That can only mean one thing.

She recognized me and wasn't happy to see me. Probably ran off to tell her dad or fiancé or whoever, that she doesn't want me as a driver. Maybe even why.

Can you say clusterfuck?

Resuming my posture, I wait for someone to come out of the house and tell me there's been a mistake. That my services won't be needed after all. Possibly run me off his property for fucking his daughter and then disappearing into thin air.

That's fine.

Clusterfuck or not, my mind is made up.

Five years ago, I started something with Claire St. James, and it's high fucking time I finish it. She can have her daddy send me away. Hell, she can get married if that's what she wants to do, but I'm not going anywhere.

No matter what or who comes out that door, I'm here.

And this time, I'm not leaving.

SEVEN

Claire

My entire life, I've been left behind.

Our mother left us when Bri and I were eleven. I remember standing in the doorway of my parent's bedroom, dry-eyed, watching her move from closet to dresser, dresser to suitcase while Bri cried, begging her not to go between each hiccupping sob while our dad sat on the edge of the bed, his back turned toward us all while he stared out the window.

Our mother never said a word. Never promised to come back. Never said she loved us. She just closed her suitcase and walked out the door.

We never saw her again.

While Bri went off after high school, attending Fashion school and snagging her dream job as assistant editor of a hot, new fashion magazine, I stayed here. Got my pharmacy tech license and took a job at the only pharmacy in town. I stayed, not because that's what was expected or demanded of me but because everyone just assumed that's what I wanted. When Bri loaded her suitcase into the back of the zippy little convertible Dad bought her for graduation, I watched her go, watched her leave me, with the same sort of detached acceptance I watched our mother walk away.

"No *My Fair Lady* without me," she whispered in my ear before pulling away from me to look me in the eye, searching my face for the pain she felt when our mother left. Like she's been waiting years for some sort of sign that I'm finally feeling what she felt, watching her leave us. Not because she *wants* me to hurt. Because she wants to feel less alone in her loss. She wants me to feel, period.

"Okay." I remember smiling. Squeezing my hands around her arms before letting her go. Waving and blowing kisses as she started her car and drove away. I always expected the loss of her to hurt. But the truth is, it didn't.

Not even a little bit.

I like to think it would've, if not for Jaxon.

What happened between us.

What he did to me.

What I *begged* him to do to me.

Waking up the morning after to find him gone confused me. The unanswered texts I sent him in the days that followed worried me. Chipped away at the paper-thin shell that held me together until I was covered in cracks, just waiting to break.

I was supposed to sit for Simon on Friday. I'd wait. Talk to him then. There had to be a reasonable explanation for why he wasn't answering me.

Friday would come, and Jaxon would apologize. Explain. Even if it was something I didn't want to hear, he'd give me a reason. I'd understand why he left without saying goodbye.

But when I got to his house to sit for Simon, Jaxon wasn't there. It was just his mother and Simon, watching cartoons in the living room.

There were moving boxes everywhere.

That's when *I* knew. Understood.

Jaxon was gone, and he wasn't coming back.

Simon and his mom were leaving too.

I went numb after that.

Been numb ever since.

I'd been infatuated with Jaxon Bennett from the first moment I saw him. Over the years, watching him with Simon, the patient, thoughtful way he spoke to him. The way he read to him. Took care of him without complaint. The way he smiled at me like we shared some sort of secret, the silly infatuation I felt grew into something more. Something deeper.

I can say I fell for Jaxon fast, or that what I felt wasn't love at all. It was lust. Crazy, hormonal, hard-bitten lust. I could say that.

But it would be a lie. The fact is, it took me years to fall in love with Jaxon Bennet but it only took a single night for that fall to break me.

My mother left me behind.

My sister left me behind.

The boy I fell in love with left me behind.

It's strange that the loss of him, the one that should hardly matter, is the one that matters most.

EIGHT

Claire

2013

By the time I get home, Bri's party has gone from just a few friends to totally insane. Like every high school party you've ever seen in a John Hughes film, crazy. I have to park three blocks away and walk back. Even so, I'm not worried about the cops showing up. Our house is on a huge lot, set back off the street and the neighborhood is patrolled by private security. The most that will happen is one of them will pull up in his golf cart and tell us to keep it inside.

Besides, we're all graduating seniors— most of us are eighteen. And the police chief's son is doing kegstands in the kitchen. We're practically untouchable.

I push my way through the front door, weaving myself through the rowdy crush of people trying to find my sister. I get waylaid by her ex-boyfriend and his merry band of jockstraps, listening while he goes on and on about how even though he dated Bri, it was really me he was into the whole time. That's about the time I start laughing and tell him he's full of shit before walking away.

I spot Bri in the living room, holding court on the couch. As usual, she's in her element. Surrounded by admirers. Laughing and talking. Flirting and teasing. It's rare that I feel jealous of her, but I feel it now. Just a twinge. On its heels follows a wave of guilt. It's not my sister's fault she's... better.

Not wanting to fight my way across the crowd, I tap out a quick text instead.

Me: I'm home.

As soon as she gets it, her head comes up and swivels, looking for me. She spots me, waving me over before pushing on the shoulder of the guy sitting beside her, telling him to move so I can sit next to her.

I shake my head and she rolls her eyes. Just because she knows I don't like parties, doesn't mean she doesn't think I'm lame.

Bri: How was
dinner? ☺

The question heats my cheeks. I want to tell her what happened. That Jaxon kissed me. More than kissed me. That he's coming over. But I don't. For all her eggplant emojis, Bri is protective of me. If she knew what happened, she'd kick everyone out, just so she can talk to me about it. And I don't want to talk about it. I'm afraid if I say anything out loud, none of it will have been real.

Me: Good.
I'll tell you
all about it
in the morning.
Going to bed.

As soon as she reads my text, she looks up at me and shakes her head. I point upward, telling her I'm just going to go upstairs. I know she means well, but watching people fawn all over her while fighting off her sloppy seconds is the last thing I want to do.

She frowns at me before looking at her phone. The text comes through a few seconds later.

Bri: Front stairs
are blocked.

Bri has throwing parties down to a science. She locks away valuable in our dad's home office. She blocks the front stairs to keep people from going upstairs. She's surprisingly responsible about it all, considering there are half-naked people running around.

Bri: No watching
My Fair Lady
without me.

Every once in a while instead of going out with friends, Bri'll stay home with me and watch movies. Her favorite is *My Fair Lady*. She says she has nothing better to do, but I think she just feels sorry for me and gets tired of getting turned down when she invites me to tag along.

I laugh, and she blows me a kiss before I turn and head for the kitchen. Tucked away in the butler's pantry is the back staircase, manned by a locked door. Like the rest of the locks in the house, it's one of those fancy ones that takes either a key or code. Handy when Bri locks herself in our Jack and Jill bathroom for hours on end.

Keying in the code, I unlock the door and head upstairs, the insanity downstairs fading to a dull roar with each step I mount. As usual, blocking the front staircase worked. No one is up here but me.

It's been about an hour since I left Jaxon's house and I haven't heard from him. To be fair, he never actually said he was coming over. He might've gotten caught up with his mom. He might've fallen asleep. He might've come to his senses and realized a girl like me isn't worth his time or effort.

In my room, I strip out of my clothes and toss them in my hamper—I was downstairs for a whole fifteen minutes, and I'm already covered in beer—debating on a shower before I decide I'm too tired. If Jaxon's not coming over, then what's the point? I settle for washing my face and brushing my teeth, pulling on an old pair pajamas.

Leaving the bathroom, I turn off the overhead lights and switch on my reading lamp. Choosing a case from the row of Blu-rays in my collection, I pop it into my player.

I'm snuggled into bed with the lights off and the movie cued, but I don't really want to watch it. What happened with Jaxon has been playing on a constant loop in my head. What he said. The way he touched me. The way his mouth felt against my neck. The strain of his hard cock, working and flexing against my throbbing center, fucking me through our clothes. Now that I'm not moving, focusing on the *next thing I have to do*, it all pushes its way to the front of my brain, so real, so vivid, I can feel my pussy start to pulse and swell. I'd be on the edge of an orgasm when we'd had to stop, and it left me feeling achy. Needy.

Closing my eyes, I let my hand slip past the waistband of my pajama bottoms, brushing between my legs, along the outside of my panties. I'm so swollen, so sensitive, the slightest touch makes me gasp. I draw my fingertips up the seam of my slit, the press of them instantly soaking the crotch of my panties...

My phone lets out a chirp, the sound of it so loud it startles me.

Expecting a *don't be lame, come back downstairs* text from Bri, my heart leaps at my throat, getting stuck there when I see a text from a number I recognize.

Jaxon: I'm outside your house.

NINE

Jaxon

I'm not sure how long I've been here. Awhile. Long enough to know I *shouldn't* be here. That I should do the right thing. Go home. She doesn't even know I'm here. Neither does anyone else, really. I could just go.

Leave her alone.

With her gone, I was able to think things through rationally. Without the feel of her against me, the sounds of her, whimpering and gasping with every stroke of my cock against the center of her, urging me on, I can see things clearly.

I'm leaving.

I'm not coming back.

I can't do this to her.

I pushed her out the back door and watched her stumble down the steps, looking as drunk and disoriented over what happened between us as I feel. I stood on the back porch and watched her cross the street to her car while my blood pounded in my ears, my arms crossed over my chest in an effort to keep myself together. Behind me, my mom walked into the kitchen, dropping her purse on the table.

For once in my life, we were over-staffed... is that Claire driving away?

Yeah. She stayed for dinner. Simon asked her to.

That's nice...

I sit with her while she eats the plate Claire put in the oven for her, half-listening to her tell me about her day. I can hear her talking, I'm even participating in the conversation, but my mind is somewhere else.

It's on Claire.

And even though I'm still telling myself to leave her alone, to let what happened be *all* that happens, I know I won't.

I know I can't.

As soon as I hear my mom's bedroom door close, I take a quick shower, using Simon's watermelon-scented shampoo because we share a bathroom and it's just easier when your five-year-old roommate uses your toiletries as bath toys. Afterward, I scrawl out a quick note with one of Simon's crayons and stick it to the fridge with one of his alphabet magnets—

Mom -
Went for a drive.
Jax

So here I am, standing on her front lawn while people I went to high school with are running around like wild animals. I'm getting a few errant, puzzled looks—like they see me but don't really believe what they're seeing. Like tomorrow morning they'll say, *I was so fucked up last night I thought I saw Jaxon Bennett.*

I've never been what you would consider social. Could never really afford to be and to be honest, it never really felt like I was missing much. What could my peers understand about my life, anyway?

I think that's what might've drawn me to Claire in the first place. Even before I started to think about all the things I wanted to do to her, I wanted to know her. Talk to her. Spend time with her. I hadn't felt that way about anyone in a long time. If

I'm completely honest, it's what prompted me to suggest we ask her to be Simon's sitter in the first place.

There've been a lot of nights I've laid awake, listening to Simon's light snore across the sea of Legos and action figures, staring at her number on my phone. Thinking about calling her. Maybe ask her out to a movie. Take her to dinner. In the end, it always seemed easier to just leave her alone. But that was before. Before I felt her tremble and sigh under my hands. Before I listened to her say the one word I've been dying to hear her say to me.

Yes.

I can't leave her alone anymore.

I don't want to.

Cursing myself, I dig my phone out of my pocket and send her a text before I can come to my senses.

Me: I'm outside
your house.

Almost immediately, a light clicks on upstairs, reminding me of what she told me earlier. That she hates it when her sister throws parties and that she usually spends her time in her room. The thought of her hunkered down, hiding away from the drunk and swarming masses like it's all some sort of natural disaster to be weathered, makes me smile.

Claire: Okay

That's it.

Okay.

I stare at my phone for a few seconds, trying to decipher the one-word text like it's an encrypted military secret when another one comes through.

Claire: Go to the kitchen

I fight my way through the house, pushing my way toward the back of it until I finally find the kitchen. Cabinet doors are hanging open. Cups and half-empty bottles scattered across the counter, despite the fact that there's a 55-gallon trash can—the kind I imagine their gardener uses to collect lawn clippings—wedged into the corner. Fighting the urge to clear the clutter, I pull a red plastic cup from a random stack, filling it with water from the tap. The police chief's kid is doing a kegstand, his buddies holding his legs steady while he does a handstand on the rim of the keg, the operator giving the tap a few pumps before thumbing the nozzle to start the flow of beer from keg to kid.

My phone buzzes again.

Claire: Backstairs are in the butler's pantry. Code for the door is 51597

What the fuck is a butler's pantry?

Feeling like a dumbass, I look around the kitchen. Spotting a door that doesn't look like it actually goes anywhere, I take a chance, shouldering my way through the tight knot of people clustered around the keg to squeeze myself through the door, barely refraining from tossing people out of my way like a deranged ogre.

I'm not really built for crowds.

I'm in a space about the size of my own bedroom. It looks like another kitchen, only smaller. Counters and cabinets on either side. A prep sink. A refrigerator.

And a door with a keypad with a red flashing light.

I key in the code, Claire sent me and the light goes green. Palming the knob I give it a turn, opening the door.

And run right into her.

Her eyes go wide. "*Oh*." She lets out a breath, her hand still latched around the doorknob, jerking her across the short distance between us.

"Shit." My hands come up, wrapping around her upper arms, holding on to her, so she doesn't plow her face right into my chest. I get the impression of baggy clothes, possibly pajamas. Her hair is up. Face scrubbed clean.

It takes considerable effort to keep my hands on her shoulders, especially when all I can do is think about shoving her against the wall and my hand up her shirt.

I need space. Distance. I move her back, away from me. Her hand detaches from the knob, and the door bangs shut behind me, leaving us in the dark. "Jaxon?"

"Yeah?" My voice sounds like I swallowed a handful of hot asphalt. Rough. Too rough. I'm going to scare her if I don't knock it off. When she doesn't follow up, I think I'm already there. She's already deciding inviting me up to her room was a bad idea. Trying to figure out a way to get me—

"I didn't think you were going to come."

I have to grit my teeth, set her away even further because the way she said *come* goes straight to my dick. "I got..." *Scared. Worried. A conscience.* Instead of telling her the truth, I lie. "Held up. With Simon. I—"

"Is he okay?"

The concern in her voice nearly undoes me, and I have to swallow hard against the lump in my throat. "Yeah...." I close my eyes even though we're standing in a dark stairwell because I can feel her breath on my neck like she's tipped her face up to look at me. I don't want to talk about Simon. I don't want to talk about my mom or how fucked up my life really is. "I'm here now."

She sighs, her shoulders softening under my hands, melting like warm butter. "I'm glad."

Jesus.

I'm in trouble.

I lower my head, opening my eyes. My sight adjusted, it's not as dark anymore. I can see the shape of her. The impression of her mouth, inches from mine, reminding me of earlier. How close she was. What it felt like to kiss her. What she tasted like. She's staring up at me, her eyes wide, like she's looking at something dangerous. Something that wants to eat her.

She has no fucking idea.

"Have you been drinking?"

I can practically hear her confusion. "What?" She shakes her head. "No—I mean, I had some cranberry juice but not—"

I give in.

Finally, let myself have *something*.

Claire.

That's the last rational thought I have, right before I kiss her.

TEN

Claire

2018

This is happening.

It's really happening.

Jaxon Bennett is my limo driver.

I'm standing on the front porch, pretending to check my purse for the essentials—ID. Cellphone. Money. Emergency Credit card—while my dad chats him up, nodding and smiling. Reaching up to clap a hand against his enormous shoulder. They're standing at the foot of porch steps, less than ten feet away and it doesn't take long to realize my father recognizes him.

... mother must be proud.

... always impressed with your dedication to Simon.

... always wondered what happened to you.

That makes two of us.

The thought makes me laugh, the sound of it bubbling past my lips and Jaxon's head snaps up at the sound. He's still wearing his sunglasses so I can't see his eyes but I don't have to see them to feel them. He nails me with a look so sharp, I can practically feel it pierce my skin.

I roll my lips over my teeth in response because I know what it sounded like. It sounded like I'm crazy. Like I'm somehow affected by his sudden and unwelcome appearance, and I'm not.

I.

Am.

Not.

"Oh, Claire." My dad spots me while I push myself across the porch. "You remember Jaxon, don't you?"

"Hello, Claire." A hand appears in front of me. A very large, very strong hand, offering to help me navigate my way down the steps.

So much for being forgettable.

I hesitate, cursing Bri and these godforsaken shoes. The only thing I want less than to touch Jaxon Bennett is for him to see me trip down the stairs like a deer on roller skates. Making up my mind, I slip my hand in his, aiming what I hope is a puzzled expression in his direction.

"I'm sorry," I say, giving him my best Grace Kelly. "Have we met?"

His hand tightens, his long, wide fingers squeezing around mine, almost hard enough to hurt. As quickly as they constrict, his fingers loosen. "See, Dr. St. James," he says on a laugh while his thumb sweeps over the soft underside of my wrist. The gentle pressure is intimate. Designed to remind me of all the other intimate things I let him do to me. It works. I suddenly can't breathe. "I told you she wouldn't remember me." He aims an easy smile at me. "You used to babysit for my… Simon." He does it again, skims the pad of his thumb over the pulse hammering away in my wrist, and it takes everything I have to keep my knees from buckling completely. I give him a blank look, silently willing myself to stand my ground.

Finally, splitting an apologetic smile between him and father, I pull my hand free from his. "I remember Simon, but I don't remember you," I say, feeling fierce and savage when I see his smile go hard around the edges. "What was your name again?"

"Jaxon." He says it carefully, like the sound of his own name is sharp against his tongue. "Jaxon Bennett."

"*Hmmm…*" I cock my head, twisting my lips like I'm trying to remember him. Finally I right my head and shrug. "Nope. Doesn't ring a bell."

"Claire—" The admonishing tone my father uses on me makes me feel like a child. A bratty, spoiled child.

Turning toward him, I lean over to give my dad a quick kiss on the cheek. "Don't wait up," I say before blading myself between the two of them, heading toward the open door of the limo where I can see Bri waiting.

"… apologize. Claire's had a rough couple of years. When Brianna left, she…"

Hearing him apologize for me makes me want to scream. Hearing him categorize my king-sized abandonment issues as *a rough couple of years* makes me want to cry. Especially since he's explaining them to the one person whose leaving hurt me the most.

I risk a look out the open door as I slide across the seat. Jaxon is looking right at me. "No apology necessary, sir. There wasn't much about me worth remembering back then."

"That certainly isn't the case now," my dad says, offering Jaxon his hand. "I'd like to thank you for your service."

"Thank you, sir." Jaxon smiles at my father and takes his hand, offering him what sounds like a rehearsed response. "Your gratitude is appreciated."

So that's what happened.

Jaxon went into the military.

Mystery solved.

"We better not lose our reservation." I look up to find Bri frowning at her cell phone. "I had to book it six months in advance."

Actually, I booked it, and it was nearly nine months ago, but I don't point that out. I'm too busy watching Jaxon. He leaves my father at the bottom of the porch steps, walking toward me at a fast clip.

"Relax, we won't be late," I say to her, still looking up at Jaxon through the open car door. His jaw is clenched tight and even though I can't see his eyes, I can feel them, dark and intense, trained on my face. He's angry. Feels rejected. Confused. Good. Now he knows what it feels like. "I'm sure Lurch is an excellent driver."

I have the satisfaction of watching his jaw go slack, right before I shut the door in his face.

ELEVEN

Jaxon

Did she just call me Lurch?

Fucking Lurch?

It would be funny if not for the fact that I'm so pissed I can barely see straight.

I didn't expect her to fall into my arms, weeping tears of joy over my safe and triumphant return but I sure as shit didn't expect her to deny even remembering me.

A polite nod. A smile. A *yes, I remember. How have you been, Jaxon?*

Yes.

A puzzled smile. A blank stare. An *I have no fucking idea who you are because nothing that happened between us was worth remembering?*

No.

Oh, hell no.

Leaving her father behind, I come at her fast, eyes locked on her with laser focus. I don't know what I'm going to do when I get to her, but I'm pretty sure it'll start with me throwing her over my shoulder and probably end with my needing bail money. She saves us both by calling me Lurch and slamming the car door in my face.

I hear her sister laugh, the sound of it punctuated by the snap of the doors being locked.

She's as smart as I remember.

Just not as sweet.

When I looked up and saw her standing there, it was like no time had passed between us at all. There she was, so goddamned beautiful I was sure her father would notice it. How seeing her again made me feel.

What it did to me.

The dress is just this side of an indecent exposure citation. Strapless. Tight and low across her tits. So short I'd bet my ride she'd flash me her ass if she bent over. Sky-high stripper heels bring the top of her head to the bridge of my nose.

But that's where it stops. Where her sister's bottle blonde hair is curled and tousled in an *I just got finished having sex* kind of way, Claire's light brown hair is swept away from her face in a simple, loose braid. Barely-there makeup. No jewelry.

The juxtapose between the package and what it's wrapped in is as confusing as it is arousing. I'm not sure if I want to cover her up with my jacket or drag her inside and fuck her. And then she looked at me like I was a vacuum cleaner salesman who'd overstayed his welcome and I had the sudden urge to turn her over my knee.

More confusion.

More arousal.

Jesus Christ, it's been a hell of a day.

The only thing that kept me steady was the fact that her father was standing right there. I like him. I've always liked him. It's usually the mother who gets left holding the bag while the father jumps ship. Claire's mom was long gone before I ever met her but I don't have to have meet her to know what I think of her. Any parent who bails out on their kid is a piece of shit, in my opinion.

Giving myself some time to cool off, I check the night's itinerary. Dinner at some swanky downtown Chicago bistro. I've taken clients there before, I know the Maître de. A string of clubs, most of which I have relationships with their heads of security—one, in particular, I served with in the Marines. Nothing crazy. Nothing dangerous.

As far as Bachelorettes go, this club crawl would've been totally uneventful, if not for the fact that the woman I've been in love with since I was eighteen years old is currently sitting in the back of my limo.

And hating my guts.

TWELVE

Claire

2013

I've never been kissed before Jaxon. Unless you count Billy Jenkins sticking his tongue in my mouth in the seventh grade on a playground dare.

Which I don't.

Not anymore.

Not with the way Jaxon is kissing me now. This is not some awkward and mildly embarrassing schoolyard fumble. This is something else.

Before tonight, I've had zero experience aside from the Billy incident, Bri's war stories and my own curious, late-night explorations under the covers. This blows all of those things out of the water. This is something else entirely.

Something hot. Desperate.

The urgent press of his mouth against mine. The way his tongue skims the seam of my lips. The way one of his huge hands wraps around my ponytail, tugging on it, angling my mouth under his so he can deepen the kiss. I let him inside, opening my mouth, a small desperate sound rippling up my throat when I do.

He growls at me—or rather against me, his mouth fused to mine so tight I can feel the vibrations of it in my chest, right before he advances. Gripping my hip, he pushes me against the wall, wedging his thick, hard thigh between my legs, pushing them wide.

Squeezed into the narrow space at the foot of the stairs, his enormous frame towering over me, I should feel crowded. Overpowered. He's easily twice my size. Big bones. Hard muscles. He's huge. All of him. I can feel the thick, rigid length of him pressed against my belly. I want what he was giving me before. I want to feel the hard press of him moving against me.

Inside me.

The hand on my hip moves, pushing under the hem of my shirt, searching for bare skin. "Claire..." he whispers my name against my mouth, his fingertips skimming the waistband of my pants giving me time to protest before he pushes past it, lower. Cupping my pussy in his hand, the heel of it pressing against the top of my mound, grinding my clit while his long, blunt-tipped fingers trace its seam through my panties. He leans into me, bringing his mouth to my ear. "You're soaked."

On the other side of the door, the light in the butler's pantry clicks on. It seeps through the cracks, illuminating his features. He's watching me, his dark eyes heavy and hooded, fused to mine, still stroking me through the thin fabric between my thighs.

I can hear people just behind the door. The fridge beside it open. Bottles clinking. People giggling. Whispering.

It looks expensive.

Should we drink it?

Fuck yeah, we're drinking it.

He's right. I am soaked. Have been since I left his house. Just thinking about it makes my pussy start to throb. I let out an answering whimper, my bottom lip caught between my teeth.

"*Shhh…*" Then his fingers push my panties to the side, their tips gliding effortlessly, pushing past my damp slit. Searching for more.

I grit my teeth as I cling to him, my hands gripping his shoulders. I make a weird noise in the back of my throat, a strange mewling sound I've never made before. I'm suddenly hot. So hot I feel my skin go taut, squeezing tight around my bones even as my insides start to tremble, liquefying from the heat.

"God, you feel so good..." he breathes in my ear, skimming his thumb over my clit, soft, feathery strokes, again and again, while a single, long finger strokes my entrance, before slipping inside, pushing deeper and deeper.

And then he stops.

Goes stiff.

The hand between my legs falls still, his finger still inside me, pressed against the barrier of my virginity.

I can feel him watching me, staring down at me. His jaw tight. Chest heaving like he's having a hard time catching his breath. "You're a virgin."

It's not a question, but I nod anyway, shame burning my cheeks.

In the butler's pantry, I hear the pop of a champagne cork, followed by a muffled, drunken cheer.

THIRTEEN

Jaxon

I knew. No matter what I've heard, no matter how many guys I've listened to spout off about how they've banged the St. James twins, I knew the truth.

Claire's a virgin.

And here I am, fingerfucking her in a dark stairwell, while drunk partiers guzzle her dad's champagne like it's Boon's Farm, not more than three feet away.

Believe it or not, that's not even the most messed up part about all this.

The messed up part is that I don't want to stop.

I want to keep going.

I want to make her come, screaming my name so fucking loud, the whole house will hear her.

There's only one thing stopping me.

I can feel how ashamed she is. Not of this—what I'm doing to her. She's ashamed that no one's ever done it before. She doesn't even have to say anything, I just know. She's embarrassed because she thinks because now that I know that no one else has ever fucked her, I won't want to either.

I'd laugh my ass off if the thought of her with someone else didn't make me want to kill something.

She's looking up at me. Waiting for me to reject her. Maybe even laugh at her.

On the other side of the door, someone starts fucking with the keypad, punching random numbers and rattling the doorknob.

Hey, what's in here?

I dunno. The Bat Cave?

Maybe Dr. St. James has a sex dungeon.

Open it. I wanna see the Bat Cave.

Fuck the Bat Cave. I wanna see the sex dungeon.

Jesus Christ.

I pull my finger out and fix her panties. I want to put it in my mouth. I want to taste her so fucking bad I have to curl my hand into a fist to keep myself in check. If having me finger her while half of our high school is running wild through her house hasn't completely freaked her out then watching me lick her off my fingers will sure as fuck do the trick.

Leaning in, I press my lips to the soft spot behind her ear, her pulse banging like a drum against my mouth. "We should go to your room," I whisper, pulling back just enough to look her in the eye.

She stares up at me, her gaze wide, chest heaving. For a second, I think she's going to tell me no. To leave. I'm half hoping she *does* because virgin or not, we both know what's going to happen if she takes me to her room.

She doesn't.

She takes me by the hand and leads me upstairs.

FOURTEEN

Claire

Jaxon Bennett is in my bedroom. He's in my bedroom and I can't even look at him for more than a few seconds without feeling a warm flush of heat wash over me because all I can think about is the fact that I can still feel his hand between my legs. His finger stroking inside me. His thumb...

At this rate I'm going to come myself into a quivering puddle, just sitting here, looking at him in three-second increments.

"Are you sure you want me here?"

I catch my lower lip between my teeth and risk another glance. He's wearing loose jeans and a collared shirt I've never seen him wear before. He showered. Shaved. Smells downright delicious—watermelons again and something else I can't put my finger on. Something that must be unique to him because whatever it is, I can't take a breath around him without feeling faint.

Meanwhile, I'm sitting here in a pair of my father's cast-off PJs, my hair thrown into a lumpy ponytail, smelling like stale beer and nervous sweat.

Life is decidedly unfair.

He's staring at me. Because he asked a question. A real question. One he expects an answer to.

Are you sure you want me here?

"Yes." The word comes out on a wobbly squeak. I clear my throat as quietly as I can and try again. "Yes."

Better but still pathetically embarrassing.

Sitting on the edge of my bed, I watch him wander around my room, lifting books to read their spines. Leaning in to look at the pictures tacked on my cork board. Dragging his finger down the row of Blu-rays on my shelf.

Having him here makes me see how juvenile it all is. Pale blue walls. White eyelet comforter. Stuffed animals. Shelves stuffed with books and movies. The N'Sync poster I hung when I was ten and never took down because Justin Timberlake.

I feel like a kid. *He* makes me feel like a kid.

"How old are you?" I blurt it out. It's a stupid question. We went to high school together. I logically know he can't be that much older than me, but there's always been something about him that has seemed almost weary. My mother would've called him an old soul.

"I turned twenty a few months ago," he says, looking at me over his shoulder. "You turned eighteen May 5th."

I look at him, shaking my head. "How did you—"

"Your friends used to tape balloons to your locker at school every year." He gives me *the smile*. The one that ties me in knots and makes me wonder what he's thinking. "Don't worry, I'm observant. Not a stalker."

"I never..." I shake my head, my tongue tripping over my teeth in an effort to get the words out. "I never thought..." If anything *I'm* the stalker. How many times have I done his family's laundry in the name of *helping out*, just so I have an excuse to touch his clothes?

Too many to be considered normal.

"And they aren't my friends—not really." I feel my brow crumple, embarrassed for some reason. "They're Bri's. I'm just—"

"Along for the ride?"

"Yeah, something like that." I laugh. Making fun of myself is something I can do. Something I'm good at. "I'm not popular. I'm more like, *popular by proxy*... if not for my sister, I'd be invisible."

"I see you just fine." He turns away from my movie shelf and faces me head on. "And I couldn't pick your sister out of a line-up."

Oh, boy.

It doesn't matter that he's already kissed me. It doesn't matter where his hands were ten minutes ago. I'm alone in my room with Jaxon Bennett, and he's looking at me like he wants... something. Something that only I can give him. This is the culmination of every late night, *lock-the-door-and-touch-yourself* fantasy I've ever had. So naturally, I have to screw it up.

"Are you... I mean, are we going to—"

Holy shit, Claire. Stop talking.

Because I never seem to listen to myself, I keep rambling.

"Is something going to happen here? Between you and me? Are you here to—"

He gives me *the smile* again. "Am I here to pop your cherry?"

Oh, my god. Don't pass out.

I nod.

"No." He turns away from me again, this time toward my bedroom door. For a crazy, hot second, I think he's decided that hacking his way through my bumbling ridiculousness isn't worth the effort. I think he's going to leave. I contemplate throwing myself in front of the door. How long can I keep him here against his will before it's considered kidnapping in the state of Illinois?

He doesn't leave.

"I'm just *here*, Claire." He reaches for the knob and very slowly, very deliberately, turns the lock. "We'll do whatever you feel ready for. Whatever you want."

"I want—"

You.

This.

Whatever *this* is.

Whatever you want.

The rest of it gets stuck in my stupid throat, and it's either stop talking or choke to death. Bri lost her virginity years ago. Why is this so hard for me?

Because you aren't Bri.

Not even close.

FIFTEEN

Claire

2018

All of Bri's bridesmaids live in Chicago, which is a few hours away, so it's just me and Bri for the first leg of the trip. We play car games we made up when were kids and talk about the wedding. I'm only half listening, a skill I developed, being her sister. Whatever she wants to do, wherever she wants to go, I'll agree. It's just easier that way.

The trip flies by. Before I know it, we're pulling in front an apartment building. As soon as we pull up, Bri's phone chirps. Giving the screen an annoyed swipe she sighs and rolls her eyes before hitting the call button on the intercom.

"You rang?" Jaxon's deep voice fills the back of the limo, and I have to tip my head down to hide the fact that I'm laughing.

If Bri recognizes his response as Lurch's tagline from *The Addam's Family*, she doesn't act like it. "Driver, I have to go upstairs for a few minutes."

"Yes, ma'am."

Almost immediately, Jaxon's door pops open, and I hear him climb out.

"Sara's having a wardrobe crisis," she says, shaking her head as the door opens.

"Want me to handle it?" I'm maid of honor, these things are my job.

"No." Bri waves her hand at me. "You stay here—" A broad, masculine hand appears in the open door. "I'll be right back."

Before I can argue, Bri's gone, leaving me alone.

The door doesn't close behind her.

Jaxon climbs into the back of the limo, claiming Bri's seat. Now he closes the door.

The limo is a late model stretch. There's enough room in here for the Chicago Bears offensive line, but I suddenly feel claustrophobic. Like I can't breathe. I aim my gaze out the window and ignore him.

"Lurch."

Against my will, the one-word question that isn't really a question draws my attention. Sunglasses off, I can see his face. He looks different. His face is leaner. Harder, making me wonder where he went. What happened to him while he was gone. What he saw while he was there.

But he's still beautiful. The way he looks at me is still the same. Direct. Intense. Like he's trying to convey everything he is, everything he feels, through the weight of his gaze.

"I apologize if I hurt your feelings," I say, flicking my gaze over his face. "I forgot your name."

The air changes between us. Thickens. Heats. Makes it hard to breathe. "No, you didn't." His tone is low. Quiet.

"Sorry." I look away, aim my gaze out the window again. "I have no idea who you are," I lie, before dismissing him completely.

"Claire."

He says my name softly, like a warning, the sound of it causes my heart to stutter and stall in my chest. Sends a flush of heat rushing through my entire body before it pools in my belly. I start counting cars as they roll past to combat the onslaught of memories.

The way his mouth followed the line of my throat, pressing and nipping its way from my collarbone to my lips.

One

His fingers, pushing past the waistband of my pajamas to brush the elastic edge of my panties before slipping inside.

Two

The heat of his fingers between my legs, the soft, deliberate trace of them along the seam of my pussy.

Three

His tongue, tracing the curve of my breast while his—

I hear the door locks engage, seconds before I feel the car rock around me as he moves closer. No longer in Bri's seat, he's sitting on the plush leather bench, right next to me. "Look at me, Claire."

His tone, sharp and angry forces me to turn in my seat. He's too close. Close enough to touch. His face inches from mine. His dark brown eyes intense, sharp enough to cut. "You know me," he says, reaching for me, cupping his hand around the back of my neck, pulling me closer. Despite his rough tone, his hands are gentle. Almost reverent. Just the way I remember them. "You remember me." His thumb traces down the line of my throat. Mouth dry, I lick my lips, inadvertently drawing his gaze to them.

I remember that I gave you my virginity and woke up the next morning to find you'd dropped off the face of the earth.

I almost say it. Instead, I channel my inner-Bri. "Are you this familiar with all your clients, Lurch?"

My words draw his eyes back to mine, and they narrow on my face. "You can call me *Lurch* all you want. It doesn't change the fact that you know *exactly* who I am and it doesn't change what happened between us."

My heart starts to race. My breath catches in my chest. "I have no idea what you're talking about."

He moves closer. "Then I guess I'm going to have to remind you," he murmurs softly, his lips brushing against mine, hand at my nape cradling my head as he tips it back to catch the press of his mouth.

I fight it for the space of a second before I'm sinking. Letting him pull me under. My lips part under his with a soft moan as his tongue sweeps in to wrap around mine, hands lifting and grabbing the lapels of his suit jacket, dragging him closer.

He groans against my mouth, his massive shoulders pressing me back into the seat, the hem of my skirt pushing up my thighs. He pulls back, his gaze, dark and intense, burrowing into mine. "Say it, Claire," he says softly, his tongue skimming my bottom lip. "Say my name."

"You'll have to tell me what it is first." I don't know why I'm pretending. Why I can't admit that I remember that night. Him. All I know is when I think about it, I hurt, and I want him hurt too.

"Careful," he growls the word at me, nips my lower lip with his teeth, ripping a gasp from my throat. "You don't want to play this game with me..." I feel his hand stroke the inside of my knee, fingers gliding upward to brush against the lace of my panties, stroking me softly. "Jesus..." he drops his head to my neck, his breath shuddering against my chest. "You always get this wet for complete strangers?"

The observation stains my cheeks, but I don't push him away. If anything, I slide lower in my seat, giving him better access. "My sister is going to be back, any minute."

He smirks at me. "Then you better hurry up and give me what I want," he says, running the length of his long fingers along the seam of my pussy, rubbing me through my panties. "Because I'm not stopping until you say my name."

Oh, my god. I'm already so close to coming it's almost embarrassing. "Is your name Jimmy?" I say, barely able to push the words out. "Did you used to work at the pizza place on 5th?"

"Close." He hooks his fingers around the crotch of my panties and jerks them to the side. "Try again."

I open my mouth to say something, but the words spin away from me on a low moan as his fingers slide inside me, his thumb finding the top of my cleft, drawing tight circles against my clit. Another rush of heat, this one pushing lower. Deeper. I'm suddenly trembling on the edge, rocking myself against his hand, trying to push myself over. Sensing how close I am, he eases up on the pressure his thumb is putting on my clit, giving me nothing more than light, feathery strokes that hold me in place. Keep me dangling.

"I went easy on you the last time we did this, Claire," he whispers in my ear. "I can keep you here all night. As long as it takes... all you have to do is say my name."

I squeeze my eyes shut and lift my hips off the seat, seeking the pressure of his hand even as I set my jaw, refusing to give him what he wants. "Jason? Were we chem lab partners?"

"I forgot how stubborn you are." The words come out on a growl, each punctuated by a curling stroke of his fingers. "You want to know what I remember?"

"Don't..." I don't want him to say it. I can't hear it because the moment I do, I'll be lost. I'll give in.

"I remember what it feels like to make you come on my cock." He keeps stroking me, every thrust hitting just the right spot. Holds me steady without sending me over. "What you taste like. How warm and sweet you are. How hard your pussy squeezed around me when you—"

"Stop. Talking." I shake my head, refusing, even as what he wants to hear threatens to push its way free.

"Say my name."

"Jaxon." His name comes out on a rush of breath, shaped around a moan.

He groans against my neck. "Again."

I tilt my head back, giving him access to my throat. "Jaxon."

He brushes his thumb, hard against my clit again, circling it slowly. "You remember me."

My legs start to tremble, my hands fisting so hard in his shirt, I can feel the stitches give. "Yes."

He picks up the pace, stroking his fingers inside me, the pad of his callused thumb quickening against the top of my mound. "Who I am? What we did?"

"*Yes.*" I'm moaning uncontrollably. It's Jaxon pumping his fingers in and out of me. His mouth on my neck. His hard cock pressed against my thigh. Making me come. "*Yes.*"

I start to fall, the walls of my pussy squeezing around his fingers, shuttering and gripping the length of them as wave after wave washes over me. He covers my mouth with his, tongue thrusting in tandem with his fingers inside me, fucking and stroking me through my orgasm.

He brings me down slowly, his dark, heavy-lidded gaze searching my face as he eases his fingers from me. Then he puts them in his mouth and sucks them clean. Fixes my panties. Straightens my skirt.

Looking at me with a mixture of tenderness and regret that feels like a knife to the chest.

"You remember me," he says softly, and the reminder breaks my heart, all over again.

"I remember waking up alone," I tell him, holding his gaze. "I remember wondering what I did to make you leave without saying goodbye." His brow crumples at my words, and I have to look away because he doesn't get to make me feel sorry. He doesn't get to be hurt.

He left me.

He didn't want *me*.

"Claire, I—"

"I remember Simon telling me you went away and then he was going away too." Thinking about Simon, my heart trembles in my chest, a quick fluttering that forces me to turn away from him completely. Aiming my gaze out the window, I pretend to dismiss him the way he dismissed me five years ago.

SIXTEEN

Jaxon

That wasn't supposed to happen. Not like that. I got into the back of the car because I wanted to talk to her. Apologize. Explain—or at least try to.

More important than all of that, I needed to ask her if she was getting married. I had to know—not that it matters. She can get married a thousand times to a thousand different guys who aren't me—it won't change a thing.

No matter what, Claire belongs to me.

Instead of asking or explaining, I go full-tilt caveman and fingerfuck her in the back of my limo because she called me Lurch and pretended not to know me.

Classy.

I knew she was fucking with me. She remembers me. She has to. Those ten hours with her were the best of my goddamned life. There's no way she could've forgotten me so easily. I knew it.

So I proved it.

Her sister and bridesmaid #1 came out of the apartment building a few minutes later, and I open the door. Help them into the car. Smile when bridesmaid #1 asks Bri where she found such a hot chauffeur. Meanwhile, I'm so strung out from Claire's taste in my mouth, the smell of her on my hand that I'm shaking and my cock is so fucking hard and swollen I have to move the seat back so I can fit *it* and me behind the steering wheel.

Not exactly how I saw this evening going.

We round up the rest of the bridesmaids, two of them, without incident and head for the restaurant listed on the itinerary. I know the place. I've taken clients there more than once. It's a neighborhood joint with a good layout. Only one dining area that's visible from the street. Two points of entry, easily covered. The maître de is willing to take bribes to sit my clients where I ask him to.

In the back, the party is already in full swing. Loud music. Bottles poppin'. Loud female voices. Laughter. I imagine Claire in the thick of it, smiling and laughing along with the rest of them, pretending to have a good time, the way she did in high school. I wonder if she's thinking about me. If she can still feel me. My fingers stroking her pussy. My tongue caressing her mouth.

Fuck.

Put that shit away, Bennett. Put it away, right fucking now.

You've got a job to do.

Dialing my phone, I make the call.

"Hey, Adain, it's Jaxon Bennett," I say when he answers the phone. "Bringing in a party of five. Need a table visible from the street."

"It's Saturday night," he wheedles, seeing dollar signs. "You know how busy we are."

"You're always busy, you money-grubbing shit," I say. Instead of taking offense he laughs, just like I knew he would. Adain knows exactly what he is and makes no apologies for it. "I'll tack on an extra benji—just put 'em by the window."

The promise of an extra hundred dollars, in addition to his usual extortion fee, perks him right up.

"You got it."

That's what I thought.

Thanking him, I hang up and re-dial, this time calling my mom.

"Hey, honey," she says, somehow knowing it's me even though the house phone doesn't have caller ID.

"Hey, Ma—"

"Simon's fine." She answers my question before I can ask it. "Playing Minecraft. How are you?"

She worries about me. Thinks my job is dangerous. I don't know how to tell her this shit is a cakewalk through Candyland compared to what I'm used to.

"It's good," I say, dipping off the freeway, to maneuver my way through downtown traffic. "Bachelorette party... It's Claire St. James."

"Claire?" She says it softly like we're trading secrets. "Simon's Claire?"

Simon's Claire. I forget that no one knows about us. What happened that night. That I took her virginity and then disappeared without a word.

"Uhhh, yeah. Got her in the back of the limo right now." I'm trying to sound casual and failing miserably. "Small world, huh?"

"She's getting married?" she says, her tone heavy with disappointment.

"Actually, I'm not entirely sure," I say, checking to make sure the volume of the music in the back of the limo is high enough to drown out the sound of my voice. "Either her or her sister."

Please let it be her sister.

"Jaxon…" My mom's voice trails off into silence. Either she isn't sure what to say or she knows that what she's about to say isn't something I want to hear. "You need to tell her."

Yup. Something I don't want to hear.

Mainly because I know she's right.

She keeps talking. "You should've told her years ago. Maybe if you'd explained—"

I'd always thought I kept my infatuation with Claire under wraps. Her observation shames me. Especially after everything I put her through. "I couldn't." I cut her off, not wanting to hear about all the ways I fucked everything up. "You know I couldn't."

"Jaxon." She says my name gently like she knows exactly what I'm feeling. Thinking. "You were just a kid. A *normal* kid with n*ormal* feelings. That didn't change just because—"

"I gotta go, Ma." I cut her off before she can say anything else. For some reason, listening to her excuse me—what I did—so easily makes me feel like shit. "I'll call and check-in in a few hours."

She sighs. "We'll be here."

I hang up the phone before she can say anything else.

SEVENTEEN

Jaxon
2013

She has no idea what she's doing to me. How goddamned *edible* she looks, sitting there, staring at me like she's waiting for me to pounce on her while she gnaws a hole in her bottom lip, her hands worrying along the hem of her pajama top.

A pajama top that is worn so thin I can see her nipples, how hard they are, every time she takes a breath—which is sporadic enough to worry me that she's going to pass the fuck out or have an anxiety attack.

Yeah, she has no idea what she's doing to me. That's the only thing keeping me here, on the other side of the room. Keeping me from lunging at her like a deranged lunatic.

I want.

That's as far as she gets before she stalled out, leaving me hanging.

I want you to leave.

I want you to hop on one foot and sing the Star-spangled Banner.

I want you to get me naked and lick every inch of me.

Stifling a groan, I hold my hands out, palms up in what I hope is a non-threatening gesture. "Claire..." I take a deep breath, let it out slowly. "I know this sounds ridiculous, considering what I just did to you in—"

She jumps up, gaze aimed at her bare feet. "I want to take a shower."

Holy fuck.

Calm your shit, Bennett. It's not an invitation for fuck's sake.

"—smell horrible." She scrunches up her nose in disgust. "Tommy Henderson spilled his beer all over me while I was looking for Bri and..." She looks up at me. "I'll be really quick." She turns, rooting around in her bed. Coming up with a remote, she aims it at the television at the foot of her bed. "You can start the movie without me—I've seen it a thousand times." She pushes a button and the screen flickers, the start menu giving way to opening credits. "Don't leave."

"Take your time. I'll be here when you get out." It would take a house fire to get me to leave at this point. And even then, my willingness to evacuate is questionable. "Can I take off my shoes?"

"You can take off whatever you want." She blurts it out, going white and then red the second it leaves her mouth. She squeezes her eyes shut. "*Jesus.*" She mutters it, shaking her head. "No wonder I'm still a virgin."

That bothers me.

The fact that she doesn't know how perfect she is. How much it's costing me to keep myself off of her. "Claire—"

"I'll be right back." Charging forward, she opens a door and disappears behind it. A few minutes later I hear the shower turn on.

Okay. Good. Maybe with her gone I can take a deep breath and wrangle my thoughts into some semblance of order.

I toe off my shoes and settle back onto the bed, back against the headboard, forcing myself to focus on the movie she turned on, instead of the fact that a very wet and very naked Claire St. James is within mere feet of me.

So much for order.

The title flashes across the screen, *Barefoot in the Park,* starring Robert Redford and Jane Fonda. From what I can tell, it's about a mismatched couple who fall in love and try to make it work, despite everything around them trying to pull them apart. Pretty soon, I'm so into it I don't even hear her come out of the bathroom.

"It's my favorite movie."

Hearing her so close jerks my attention away from the screen. She's standing near the edge of the bed, wearing nothing but a towel, her hair piled on top of her head. Skin still damp. Warm.

I should look away. Be a gentleman.

I can't.

I want to but I can't take my eyes off her.

"Nothing in their relationship goes right." She keeps talking. Looking at the screen, watching Redford and Fonda argue. "They don't belong together, and they know it... but they keep trying. They don't give up." She looks at me, her face cast in shadows by the soft glow of the lamp on her nightstand. "They stay."

They stay.

That's when I get it.

That's when I understand the full magnitude of that I'm going to do to her. What my being here, in her bed, means.

I'm going to take something from her I can never give back and then I'm going to leave her.

Get the fuck up and leave.

Right now.

Don't do this to her.

Don't you fucking do it.

I'll come clean. About everything. I'll solve the great mystery of Jaxon Bennett, and then it'll be over. It'll be out of my hands because she won't want me anymore. She'll realize I'm not the type of guy that a girl like her should be with.

Give herself to.

She'll tell me to get out and as impossible as it might seem for me to get up and walk away, that's what I'll do. I'll walk away before I do something I can't take back.

"Claire..." I shake my head, trying to clear it. "I need to—"

She shakes her head at me. "You said whatever I wanted. Whatever I'm ready for."

I close my eyes, try to work up the will to push myself up and off the bed.

Out of here.

I need to get out of here.

I can't do this to her.

"I know what I said but—" The bed shifts under me, seconds before I feel her straddle my hips. The press of her knees against my outer thighs. The weight of her settling in my lap. My dick goes rock hard so fast the sudden loss of blood flow to my brain makes me dizzy.

"*Fuuuck*..." The curse comes out on a groan, my hands coming up to settle on her hips, pulling her even closer, gripping the towel tight around her. "Claire…"

I feel the press of her breasts against my chest. Her breath on my face and I open my eyes to find her close, our mouths within an inch of each other.

"I'm not good at this," she says. "I'm not my sister. I don't know how to flirt. How to tease." She rocks her hips against me, a soft, desperate whimper humming in her throat. "But I know how to ask for what I want." She sits up and loosens the top of the towel, letting it fall so it can pool around her waist. "I've decided this is no different."

She's perfect.

Fucking perfect.

So perfect, I have to touch her to convince myself that she's real. Reaching up, I cup a hand around one of her breasts, brushing my thumb against its nipple. It stiffens instantly, and my cock gives a hard jerk into the juncture of her thighs and her breath catches in her chest at the feel of me pressed against her.

Encouraged by my response, she smiles.

"I want you to kiss me," she says softly, leaning in to brush her lips against mine. "I want you to touch me like you did earlier."

"Are you sure?" Jesus, I sound like an animal. Like I'm seconds away from taking her, regardless of her answer. "You need to be sure."

"Yes." She pulls one of my hands free, sliding it across the top of her thigh. She kisses me, guiding my fingers along the inside of them until they hit the hot, silky center of her. "I'm sure. And this time, I don't want you to stop."

EIGHTEEN

Claire

I'm not sure what happened.

All I know is that somewhere between turning on the shower and turning it off, I decided that I was tired of waiting.

Waiting for something to happen to me.

Waiting for someone to notice me.

Want me.

Not just something. Not just someone.

Jaxon.

I want him and I'm tired of waiting, so I can go out there and wait for something that might never happen or I can go out there and *make* it happen.

Take what I want.

Instead of putting on the fresh pair of pajamas I wrapped myself in a towel and forced myself to leave the bathroom.

He's watching the movie. So involved he doesn't even know I'm standing here. He looks like a giant, stretched across on my full-size bed, bare feet hanging over the foot of my mattress. His head propped up on pillows so he can see the television perched on my dresser.

Downstairs, the party is still raging. A hundred newly-graduated high school seniors, yelling and laughing. Music thumping. The occasional sound of breaking glass. Bri's going to have a mess to clean up in the morning. Or rather, *I'll* have a mess to clean up while she nurses a hangover. I'll be angry about it tomorrow but right now, I don't care.

All I care about is this. The fact that Jaxon Bennett is in my bed and the door is locked. That he's finally noticed me.

"It's my favorite movie," I say because I have to say something. I can't just stand here, watching him watch television.

He looks at me and what I see on his face makes the rest of it seem so easy. He wants me. He wouldn't be here if he didn't.

But he won't make the first move. I know he won't. I'm not sure if it's because I'm barely eighteen or if it's because he's afraid that it'll make things weird because I babysit Simon or because I'm a virgin. Maybe it's all three. I don't know and I don't care.

This is happening because I'm tired of waiting.

I climb on to the bed and straddle his hips, my bare pussy pressed against the hard bulge of his cock.

"*Fuuuck*." He groans it, his hands coming up to grip my hips, pulling me closer, grinding himself against me through the rough fabric of his jeans. "Claire…"

"I'm not my sister." I lean into him, planting my hands on either side of his head. "I don't know how to flirt. How to tease," I whisper, my mouth inches from his. "I don't know how to flirt. How to tease." I rock my hips against him, loving the way he groans, deep in his throat, at the contact. "But I know how to ask for what I want."

I sit up and take a deep, bracing breath, like I'm about to jump off a cliff. Loosening the top of the towel, I let it let it fall. "I've decided this is no different."

His lids lower, his dark gaze going soft and hungry. Like he can't help himself, Jaxon reaches up to cup a hand around my breast, his calloused thumb brushing over my nipple, stiffening it instantly, my breath catching in my throat when I feel his cock give a hard jerk between my thighs. Leaning into him again, I brush my mouth against his. Tell him I want him to kiss me. Touch me. And this time I don't want him to stop.

"Are you sure?" He reaches up to loosen my hair, letting it fall around us. "You need to be sure."

Am I sure? Wanting Jaxon Bennett is the only thing I am sure of. The only thing I know is real and true.

"Yes." I take his hand and guide it up the inside of my thigh, a soft moan pushing out of my mouth when I feel his fingers brush against the heat of me. "I'm sure. And this time, I don't want you to stop."

"Thank god," he groans, his hand shifting under mine, his thumb skimming up the center of me, pushing past my folds to brush against my throbbing clit. "Come here, Claire." He sweeps his thumb against me, again and again, until I'm shuddering and rocking against the pressure of his hands between my legs. "Let me kiss you."

I lean into him again, lowering my mouth to his and he groans softly when I part my lips, letting his tongue inside to tangle with mine. The hand on my hip grips the towel pooled around my waist and gives it a rough, impatient jerk before dropping it on the floor.

"I don't want to hurt you," he says, pulling his mouth from mine, his breath harsh and ragged against my neck. "I have to make sure you're ready. Go slow." My impatient groan makes him laugh. "Greedy girl…" The hand on my hip reaches lower, follows the curve of my thigh to brush the seam of my pussy from behind. "Do you trust me?"

"Yes." I'm half out of my mind, my hips rocking against the pressure of his thumb on my clit. The feel of his fingers teasing my entrance from behind as maddening and it is arousing. "Please, Jaxon. I need—"

His long, wide finger enters me from behind and I gasp when I feel it press against the barrier of my virginity.

"*Ohhh,*" I moan, the sudden, heavy pressure of his finger inside me almost more than I can bear. Within the space of a breath, I'm so close to coming I can feel my whole body begin to shake. "Jax—"

"Shhh…" He starts to move inside me, stroking me, slow and deep, pushing against me. Stretching me. "It's okay." He pulls out of me and when he pushes in again, it's with two fingers. "I want you to come, Claire. I want it to be good for you." I make a strange sound in the back of my throat when he starts to move again—half whimper, half gasp—the heat of it, spirals down my spine to pool between my thighs.

He adds another finger. "Shit," he growls when I let out a sharp gasp, teetering on the border between pleasure and pain. "Are you okay?" He goes still. "Am I hurting you?"

Yes, but not enough to make me what to stop. It hurts, but not as much as it feels good. "Don't stop," I say softly, leaning down to lick at his mouth, his slightly parted lips, loving the way he groans my name. "Please, Jaxon, I don't want you to stop."

"Jesus…" He groans softly. Starts to move again, in and out of me. "You're so fucking tight." Each stroke pushing me. Stretching me, until the pain fades and I'm panting and moaning, my hips rocking against the hot, unrelenting pressure of his fingers fucking me. Getting me ready.

The orgasm hits me fast and hard. "*Ohmygod,*" I cry out, my hands fisting in the pillow on either side of his head, while my pussy flexes and clenches around the fingers he has buried inside me.

Before I have time to catch my breath, Jaxon pulls his fingers out and lifts himself up to take my mouth in the kind of kiss that leaves you breathless, his mouth devouring me, slanting against mine, again and again, his tongue licking and swirling until I'm dizzy and everything tilts.

Suddenly, I'm under him, his hips between my thighs, his hands pressed into the bed on either side of my head, holding himself up to keep from crushing me.

"Again." He whispers it in my ear before pressing his lips against the soft skin behind my ear. "I want you to come again," he says, his mouth and tongue, licking and kissing their way down the length of my throat. My collarbone. Between my breasts. Capturing one in his hand he cups it, circling its swollen nipple with his tongue before capturing it between his lips, sucking and nipping it with his teeth until I'm gasping and moaning.

"Jaxon, please…" I whimper, eyes closed, the back of my head dug into the pillow. "I need—" I don't know what I need. All I know is I feel empty. Achy. My skin is too tight. Too hot. I lift my hips off the mattress, grinding my pussy against any part of him I can reach.

More.

I need more.

NINETEEN

Jaxon

I know this is wrong. I know I owe her more than what I'm giving her. What I'm going to do to her. I know that. But I can't stop. I want her too much. I've wanted her for too long and it's done something to me. Something I might be ashamed of if I think about it too much or too long.

I've buried it, this insatiable need for her, for so long that now that the dam is broken I'm being swept away by it. Pulled under, to a dark place where reason and sensibility can't find me. A place where I know this is wrong but I can't stop. Not with her moaning my name. Her fingers laced through my hair. Telling me she needs me as much as I need her.

Her hips come off the bed, her wet, swollen pussy grinding against my abs and I'm almost undone. The only thing that keeps me from jerking my pants down and burying myself inside her is the fact that this is her first time and I want to make it good for her. I want her to remember this. Me. Because this is the only time I'll have her. By morning it'll all be over and not long after that, Claire will regret she ever knew me.

So I have to go slow. Take my time.

Make it count.

Reaching down, I grip her hip. Push her flat against the bed while I lick my way down her torso. Along the soft curve of her belly. The top of her cleft. "Claire?" I brush my lips against her and she whimpers, instinctively pushing herself against my mouth, looking for more. "Has anyone ever licked your pussy before?"

I know the answer. I know I'm the only one. That no one has ever touched her before me, but there's a fucked-up part of me that needs to hear her say it. Admit that I'm the first.

"No." The word comes out on a ragged breath. "No one…"

I lift my head and look up the length of her. She's shaking, looking down at me. Eyes gone dark and cloudy.

"Do you want me to stop?" I will if she wants me to. Part of me hopes she says yes because that's the only way either of us gets to walk away from this thing intact.

"Again." The word sounds like its being torn from her throat, her hand reaching down to grip the back of my neck. "Please… again."

Fuck. Yes.

Planting my hands on either side of her, I grip her thighs, holding them open so I can run my tongue up the length of her, pushing past her slick folds to lick the warm, sweet honey underneath. Again and again, licking and sucking at her tender flesh until she's writhing beneath me.

"*Jaxon…*" Her hips come off the bed, pushing her pussy against my mouth. "*More…*"

Pushing my tongue deep, I find her clit and start to suck her off. Hard, greedy pulls until I'm drunk on the taste of her. The throbbing pulse of her clit on my tongue.

Making room for my hand, I slide three of my fingers into her wet pussy and she moans my name, deep in her throat when I start to fuck her, opening my fingers. Stretching her pussy. Getting her ready for my cock.

"*Ohhh.*" The hand in my hair grips tight, her thighs breaking free of the grip I have on them to slam closed around my head. "*I'm…*" She starts to come, her pussy trembling and flexing around my fingers.

Not giving her time to recover, I sit up to kneel between her thighs. "I want to fuck you, Claire." I skim my thumb up the wet, throbbing center of her. "Tell me now if—"

"Yes." She reaches for me, her fingers fisting in my shirt to pull me over her. "Yes, please."

I close my mouth over hers and she parts her lips for me, her tongue sweeping into my mouth, a soft moan breaking free when she tastes herself on my tongue.

The hand in my shirt starts to pull. Up over my head and I shift just enough to get rid of it, her hands on the waistband of my pants even before it hits the floor. Clawing at the button of my jeans. Pulling it open to make room for her hands.

I tear my mouth away from hers. "Claire." I groan her name. Finding her gaze in the dark I look down at her while reaching down to close a hand over her wrists. "That's probably not a good idea."

"Why?" she pants up at me, her breath warm and broken on my chest.

"Because I'm so hard my ears are ringing and if you touch me, I'll probably come all over you," I say, telling her the truth—well, part of it, anyway. The whole truth is that I'm six-foot-seven and everything about me is built to scale. I don't want her to get her hands on me and get scared or start to worry about how I'm going to fit. I'm worried enough for the both of us.

"Oh." She flashes me a smile in the dark. "Okay." She pulls her hands away, smoothing themselves up my ridged abs. Across my pecs. The slopes of my shoulders. I lean into the pressure of her hands. The feel of her skin against mine building a humming buzz in my head, making it hard for me to think about anything except getting inside her.

Sitting up again, I reach into my pocket to pull out one of the condoms I brought with me. When I catch her watching me I grin down at her. "I told you, I believe in being prepared for all possible contingencies."

She laughs quietly while I finish the job she started, pulling my pants down around my hips, dragging them down my legs so I can kick them off completely.

Tearing the condom open, I fit it over the head of my cock and roll it on, my hands shaking so bad I can barely get the job done.

I'm about to ask her if she's absolutely sure when she reaches for me. "Come here," she whispers, making a soft, satisfied sound in the back of her throat when I stretch out over the length of her, bracing myself up on my elbows so I don't crush her.

"I'll go slow," I say pressing the head of my cock against her entrance.

She nods up at me, eyes wide. Fingers digging into the straining muscles of my back. "I trust you, Jaxon."

Those four words wreck me. Remind me that this is wrong. What taking her will make me. What it will do to her when she realizes that I left her. I'm seconds away from bolting off the bed and out the goddamned door, wearing nothing but a condom.

But then she tilts her hips under mine and the head of my cock sinks into her and she moans my name.

And just like, I'm lost.

TWENTY

Claire

2018

I realize, at least on some level, that I'm not being completely fair. If I allow myself to remember what happened between us objectively, I can admit that I was the one driving the bus. I was the one directing traffic. I was the one who made it all happen.

But that doesn't change the fact that he made me feel.

I know that sounds stupid. I barely knew Jaxon. He never promised me anything. Never told me loved me. Never planned for the future. Our entire relationship spanned the space of a single night.

But that night felt more real to me than anything I'd ever experienced before. I felt like myself. I felt like Jaxon saw me. Who I really am, not who I pretended to be.

The lesser twin.

The dutiful daughter.

The one who always gets left behind.

Me.

"He's hot."

"Who's hot?"

I look up away from the window to see Bri give her friend, Helena, a puzzled look. Friend is a stretch. Helena is more of a co-worker. They're both junior editors at *Swoon,* a local fashion magazine.

I don't even have to look at her to know who she's talking about. She's talking about Jaxon.

I think about the two of them together and feel sick. She gorgeous. Auburn hair. Big, brown Bambi eyes. Killer rack.

Sitting next to her, I feel like a nun.

A pasty-faced, flat-chested nun.

"The driver." Helena tilts her champagne flute at the privacy partition. "Fucking. Hot."

"He's like seven feet tall," Bri says, wrinkling her nose. Tall guys have never been her thing.

"I know." Helena shoots a predatory grin around the interior of the car, staking claim.

"And I'm going to climb him like a jungle gym."

Say my name.

I press my knees together self-consciously. My body's still humming from the orgasm Jaxon gave me.

Despite the fact that it was reckless of me to let him touch me—reckless and stupid—I want him to do it again.

Why? So he can break your heart again. Spent the night making you feel and want things you never thought possible, just so he can disappear again. Make you feel like maybe you're worth sticking around for, just to get the rug jerked out from under you.

No. It's not worth the risk.

"Finish your drinks, ladies," Jaxon's deep voice, booms through the speakers. "We're pulling up to the restaurant."

Bri and her friends start to shout.

WHOO, GIRL'S NIGHT!

BEST NIGHT EVER!

WE'RE GETTING LAID TONIGHT!

Seconds later the limo pulls over, and I hear Jaxon climb out of the car. I watch him pass by the long, tinted window, moving toward the back of the car before he opens the door and his hand appears in the wedge. One by one, he helps Bri and her friends from the car. I can hear them on the sidewalk, squealing and laughing. Having the time of their lives.

Meanwhile, I'm drowning.

"Claire."

I look up to see Jaxon's face in the doorway. His gaze unflinching. Direct. Worried.

Fuck that. He doesn't get to worry about me. Pretend he cares. Because he doesn't. He made that perfectly clear the night he fucked me and then left me without so much as a goodbye.

Without answering, I down the rest of my champagne and toss the empty flute onto the leather seat beside me.

Scooting across the seat, I ignore his hand, climbing out of the car on my own. It's awkward, but I manage. As I walk past him, he snags my arm, pulling me back to press his mouth to my ear. "I'm sorry, Claire." Like he can read my mind, he gentles his grip on my arm. "I never meant to hurt you I never wanted to—"

It happens again. The rollercoaster feeling only he can give me.

Don't trust. Don't feel.

Not worth the risk.

I pull my arm from his grip and shake my head.

No, Claire.

"I don't believe you."

TWENTY-ONE

Jaxon

I knew I was going to hurt her. That what was happening between us was important—not just because she was a virgin, but because afterward, lying next to her, I wanted to stay. Be with her.

I was ready to throw everything away for her. I *wanted* to. And that made her dangerous.

I thought about waking her up, telling her everything I should've told her the night before. Tell her that I was leaving. Make her understand that I didn't have a choice. But making her understand would require the truth, and in the cold light of day, I lost my nerve because the thought of her looking at me, thinking about what happened between us with regret, killed me.

So I left. Told myself it was okay because she'd get over me. Move on. Find a good guy. One who had more to offer her than a fucked up past and a life of waiting for me to come home. Because I had to leave. No matter what I wanted, laying there with her in my arms, I knew I had to go. I never had a choice.

I told myself that by walking away, I was doing right by her and I believed it.

My reasons don't matter. Neither does the fact that leaving her behind was the hardest thing I ever had to do.

I hurt her.

And that makes me the wrong guy for her.

Wrong or not, I looked at her, standing in front of me on that porch, and I wanted her. Realized I never really stopped—and even though she hates me, she wants me too.

I saw it on her face when she looked up at me. Jerked her arm from my hand. She likes how seeing me again makes her feel. My hands on her. Inside her. But she doesn't trust me. Might never trust me again.

I don't believe you.

Too fucking bad.

I'm the one who broke her.

I know that.

But I'm the only one who can put her back together.

I know that too.

There's only one way I can do that.

Tell her the truth.

You tell her the truth and it's over. She'll never look at you the same way again. She'll regret everything that happened between you. She might even blame you. Think it was your fault…

Maybe.

Maybe she'll hear the truth about me and tell me she never wants to see me again. But she needs to know. I owe her that much after the hurt I caused.

TWENTY-TWO

Claire

They're having the time of their lives. Drinking and laughing. Hanging out of the moon-roof. Flashing pedestrians (now I understand why Bri insisted on strapless dresses). Horns are honking. People are yelling and howling at them from passing cars. I'm almost certain we're going to get pulled over.

"Claire."

Jaxon's voice over the intercom barely held above a whisper.

"Answer me, Claire." It irritates me, the way he thinks he can tell me what to do. Almost as much as it turns me on. What irritates me the most is that after five years, he still has that kind of power over me.

I jab the call button with my finger. "What?"

"I need to talk to you. I—"

Just then, Helena drops down onto the seat they're all standing on. "Hey, Driver," she says loudly, jerking her top up over her exposed breasts.

I can practically hear Jaxon sigh. "Yes, ma'am?"

She grins at me and winks. "We want to go to Nina's."

As soon as she says it, I feel my face catch fire. Nina's is a sex shop downtown. Half urban legend, half rite of passage, it's the place every kid in Chicago talked about being old enough to get into. When you turned twenty-one, you went drinking. When you turned eighteen, you went to Nina's.

I've never been.

"I'm sorry, but it's not on the itinerary," Jaxon says, his tone making his polite refusal sound like *fuck no*.

"Don't be that way," Helena shoots me a sly, *watch me work* kind of smile. "We want to put on a lingerie show for you."

She winks at me, and I think about jamming my thumb in her eye socket. The only thing that stops me is the fact that she'd probably look sexy with an eye-patch.

"An unscheduled stop is against the rules..." Jaxon's tone purrs over the speakers. "But I suppose we can make an exception."

TWENTY-THREE

Jaxon

Pulling into the parking lot, I recognize that this is probably a mistake. We keep itineraries for a reason. I should be driving them to the first stop on their club crawl. Instead, I'm pulling into the dark parking lot of a seedy, downtown sex shop.

Not my finest moment.

But I need to talk to Claire, and I doubt I'll get the chance once we're parading from club to club.

When I open the back of the limo, I'm not surprised by what I see. A half-dozen empty champagne bottles littering the floorboard. Glitter everywhere. Someone's underwear on the seat.

"Those are mine." The redhead pops out of the back of the car with a leer. Reaching back, she snags them off the seat and turns to tuck them into the front pocket of my suit. "You can keep them."

I offer her a smile in return because pissing her off is only going to take time and energy away from Claire, neither of which I have to spare. "Thanks," I say, moving her out of the way so I can help the rest of them out of the car.

They're totally faced. The tops of their dresses askew. Hair wind-blown from hanging out of the moonroof. Makeup starting to slide off their faces.

And then there's Claire.

She lets me help her out of the car this time, her gaze dropping to the purple lace G-string sticking out of my pocket, before looking away completely.

Herding them across the parking lot, I open the door and usher them across the threshold before posting up at the door. Nina's is split into two separate areas. The ground floor is well-lit and spacious. Clean. Separated into areas of interest. Relatively safe. Like Target—if Target sold 12-inch strap-ons and played porn audio tracks over their PA system.

The basement is where the real shit goes down. Growing up in Chicago, you hear stories. Sex shows. Private auctions. Orgies.

Fetish dens. Once upon a time, I was as curious as any other horny teenage boy— and then in the blink of an eye, I was too old for that shit. Too tired. Too jaded.

"Thirty minutes, ladies," I tell them, leaning against the wall, watching them scatter like buckshot around the store. The redhead heads straight for the rack of corsets and crotchless panties and starts loading up, giving me a long, lascivious look. "Everybody finds something to try on," she says loudly. "I promised Driver a lingerie show."

I stand there for a few minutes, watching the scramble, scraps of lace and silk, flying every which way. As soon as Claire hustles down the hall with a few hangers, I turn around and lock the door, flipping the sign from open to close.

"You can't do that," The woman behind the counter says, scowling at me.

"Sure I can." I pull out my wad of cash and slide her some bills across the counter-top. "For thirty minutes." If there's anything I've learned working the private sector, it's that everything and everyone has a price.

The money disappears in a flash. "Twenty."

I tilt my head, so I can see the bank of security monitors mounted under the counter. I see Claire on the screen marked #5. Reaching over, I switch it off. "Make it fifteen."

She smirks at me, giving me a long look from head to toe. "Whatever you say, cowboy—but if she starts screaming, I'm calling the cops."

TWENTY-FOUR

Claire

I have no intention of trying any of this stuff on. I grabbed a few random items off the rack made a beeline for the changing room so I'd have an excuse to sit in a quiet room by myself for a few minutes. I walk down the long row of changing rooms.

Choosing one, I push the door open and flip on the light to reveal what looks like a 5x5 closet, complete with vinyl bench, mirror and door lock. There's a box of wet wipes on the floor next to the bench.

I don't even want to think about what goes on in these rooms.

Behind me, I can hear Bri and her friends laughing and shouting. Even without an audience, they're putting on a show.

No. They have an audience.

They have Jaxon.

Stepping through the open door, I turn and shut myself in, sagging a little bit against its frame. Eyes closed, I take a deep breath. Let it out slowly. I do it again. And again.

I want to go home.

I want to go back to pretending that Jaxon Bennett doesn't exist. That what happened *didn't* happen.

No, you don't, you big liar. What you want *is for Jaxon to come back here and —*

Someone knocks on the door I'm leaning against, the sound and feel of it reverberating through my bones. Like my filthy thoughts brought him to life, I open it to find Jaxon on the other side.

I slam it in his face.

I hear him sigh, the sound heavy with frustration and something else. Something sad. "Claire — open the door. Please."

It's not locked. He could open the door if he wanted. He doesn't even try. I twist the knob in my hand, popping the latch before backing away. Jaxon pushes it open wide enough to let himself in before shutting us in together.

"What do you want?" I say, wrapping my arms around myself, hangers full of lingerie still hanging from my fingers. I keep forgetting how big he is. How much space he occupies. I put as many feet between us as possible, backing myself into a corner but it's not enough. I need more.

I need mountains and oceans between us. Continents and eons. I need him to disappear again, this time forever because that's the only thing that's going to keep me from him. The only way I won't fall again. Knowing he has that kind of power over me scares me a little. I'd forgotten how easily he can pull me under.

"I want to explain." He takes the hangers from me, doesn't even look at what's on them before tossing them on the bench seat. "I want you to give me a chance to explain." He steps into me, and I retreat. I should feel crowded. Overwhelmed. I should be screaming at the top of my lungs.

I don't.

I feel achy. Needy. Weak.

"*I'm leaving.*" I don't know what's happening, but it's not what I expected. What I thought. I thought... I shake my head. What I thought doesn't matter. All he wants is to clear his conscience. "That's all you had to say, Jaxon. All it would've taken—*I'm leaving.*"

"I know." His shoulders slump, and his head tips forward eyes squeezed shut. "*I know*... I should have said something, but I was afraid if—"

"That I wouldn't let you fuck me if I knew you were going to take off on me." I finish his sentence for him, feeling the same fierce satisfaction I felt earlier when I slammed the car door in his face.

His eyes blink open, and he stares at me for a moment before they narrow, his jaw snapped tight. "No, I—"

"Because I would've, you know." I lay it all out, too angry to think about what I'm saying. "I would've let you do anything you wanted to me, even if I'd known I was never going to see you again. That's how crazy I was about you." My voice breaks, the sharp pieces of it cutting me wide open.

The truth tumbles out, too fast for me to snatch it back and I stare up at him, wide-eyed, praying to god he thinks I'm crazy. That I didn't mean it.

He steps closer, and I counter, trying to get away but only succeeding in bumping into the mirrored wall behind me.

"Are you getting married?" he says softly, angling his head even further. I have to jack my neck all the way back just so I can keep looking at him.

I feel myself blink, slow and stupid, like some blinded animal. "Married?" I finally say, shaking my head like I don't understand his language. "You want to know if I'm getting *married*? Now?" I can feel my anger rising to near epic proportions. "You're asking *now*? After what you did to me in the—"

He growls at me, his hands clamping over my bare shoulders to haul me against him, even as his mouth crashes down. His tongue brushes against my lower lip, licking and teasing its way inside to tangle with mine. I whimper in response, the fight leaving me the second his lips meet mine. I'm lost.

Floating and spinning, the only things keeping me from drifting away is the weight of his mouth. My hands on his chest, fingers curling into the lapels of his suit jacket. His hand in my hair, his rough fingers tight against my skull, while his other slips to my hip, holding me tight, letting me feel the hard length of his cock between us. I forget about how insulted I am. How much he hurt me. Keeps hurting me. All I can remember is this. How good he felt, moving inside me. How much I wanted him.

Still want him.

The thought sends a rush of heat through me, so hard and fast I feel like I'm spinning. I slip a hand between us, lower and lower until my fingertips are grazing along the length of his rigid cock.

He groans, flexing his hips into my hand, again and again. I tighten my grip, sweeping my thumb over the engorged head of his shaft until I feel pre-cum seep through the fabric of his pants.

"*Fuck...*" Tearing his mouth away, he glares down at me. "Answer the question—are you getting married?"

I keep giving in to him. I keep letting him in.

Giving him what he wants. Every time.

I feel my jaw set itself in a mutinous jut. "Does it matter?"

He doesn't even hesitate.

"Nope." I feel the hand on my hip start to tighten, gathering the fabric of my skirt. "Not even a little bit."

TWENTY-FIVE

Jaxon

It matters.

The thought of her with someone else—getting married. Having babies. Growing old with someone who isn't me, matters.

It does.

It *fucking* matters.

Just not the way it should.

Instead of backing me up and slowing me down, the thought of her belonging to someone else pushes me into a dark place.

A place where I *have* to have her.

Mark her.

Own her.

"Claire," I growl at her, low and tight in my throat, even as I'm reaching down, fisting my hands around the hem of her dress, jerking it up, exposing her black lace panties. She doesn't stop me. Doesn't pull away. She just stares up at me, her hand gripping and stroking me through MY pants. "Be sure."

She pushes her hand into the waistband of my pants, shoving them down around my thighs, freeing my hard, thick cock completely. "I am."

I press my hand into the juncture of her thighs, fingers trailing up the seam of her pussy. Wet. She's so fucking wet she's practically dripping. The feel of her against my hand is electrifying.

She's here.

She's with me.

Belongs to me.

Control shattered, I jerk her panties to the side so hard I hear them rip. Shifting my hands, I slide them under her ass, lifting her. Opening her.

Stepping into the space between her thighs, the head of my cock slides into her, just past her entrance and immediately starts to throb. I can already feel an orgasm barreling down on me, tightening the small of my back. "I don't have a condom." It's been too long. I forgot how good being inside her feels.

Claire wraps her legs around me, digging her heels into my ass, urging me closer. Deeper. "I don't care."

Christ. I'm going to come. Soon. Too soon to make it good for her.

Gritting my teeth, I thrust deep, pinning her to the wall with my cock, my throat locked around a gruff shout, shaping it into a low groan. She gasps, her eyes going wide, hands fisting in the front of my shirt. I'm still wearing my shirt. My jacket. Someone walks by, talking on their phone, mere feet from where we're standing, looking for an empty dressing room. I forgot to lock the door.

I don't fucking care.

Using my hips to hold her in place, I hook my hands around the front of her dress and jerk it down, exposing her breasts. My dick gives a hard twitch and she moans. Her mouth opens slightly, and she begins to pant. Eyes closed, she starts to move, working her hips against mine.

Shit.

Lowering my hands, I grip her hips, holding her still. "I want to make you come first." I whisper it in her ear, tightening my hold on her when she tries to work her hips again. "Claire." My sharp tone jerks her eyes open. She seems surprised to see me. "Put your tits in my mouth."

Surprised or not, she does what I say, pushing her breasts together with her hands, lifting them up to my mouth like an offering. Like a starving man, I lower my head, taking a hard nipple into my mouth, sucking and nipping at it until it's swollen and throbbing on my tongue. I give the other one the same attention, alternating between them, while I shift my hold on her hips, sliding my thumb past her juice-slicked folds to press against the top of her mound. I don't tease. I don't play. I stay buried inside her, rocking my hips against hers, little pulses that stimulate her core until she's right where I need her to be.

"Jaxon, I need you to fuck me." She whimpers, her hips fighting the grip I have on them. "Please..."

I run my tongue between her breasts. "Not yet," I growl, nipping at her nipple with my teeth before sucking it into my mouth. Lifting my gaze, I find her looking down at me, watching me lick and suck her, her eyes the color of lake water, her gaze dark and heavy, bottom lip caught between her teeth in an effort to keep from moaning. It reminds me of that night.

Our first night.

Me, pinning her against the wall in that dark stairwell, my fingers stroking her pussy. Her clit. Her fast, uneven breath against my chest.

I almost come inside her right then and there.

I can't hold out anymore.

Nailing her to the wall with fast, deep strokes, I finally let myself fuck her. Pound my hips against hers so hard I'm sure we're going to tear it down. That the whole building is shaking around us.

"Come on me, Claire," I say, not even sure I'm whispering anymore. "Come on my—"

She moans so loud I lunge up, covering her mouth with mine so I can swallow the sounds of her orgasm.

Mine.

She's fucking *mine*.

I start to come, my dick pumping and jerking. My balls contracting and releasing, emptying themselves inside her. She comes again, her tight pussy locking around me, pulling me deeper. Milking me as aftershock after aftershock hit us both.

Sensibility creeps in. I should've pulled out. Stopped. Thought about what I was doing. I'm clean. I know I'm clean, but I could get her pregnant.

I know better. I *fucking* know better...

But as soon as I think it, I realize the thought of getting Claire pregnant doesn't scare me. Not like it should.

Not at all.

TWENTY-SIX

Claire

Jaxon turns, setting me down on the vinyl bench behind us, fixing his clothes first before kneeling in front of me. Picking up the package of wet wipes, he pulls a few free.

He looks up at me. He looks contrite. Lost. I open my legs, giving him access. He tips his face downward, concentrating on running the wet wipe along the inside of my thigh, cleaning me up.

"I'm sorry, Claire." He shakes his head. "I shouldn't have done that—and earlier in the car. I shouldn't have done that either." He looks up at me for a second, his gaze skimming over mine without taking hold. "I just..." His jaw goes tight, brow lowering slightly. He looks down again, redoubling his efforts. "I'm clean. I get tested. I haven't been with anyone for a while—I would *never* jeopardize you like that."

"I know," I say, scowling down at his bent head. When he doesn't answer me, I sigh. "Jaxon, look at me."

He gives in and looks up, his gaze settling on my cheek.

"You didn't do anything—at least not anything I didn't want you to do to."

His expression doesn't change.

"I'm on the pill." I say it because I think I figured it out. That's what this is. He came inside me, and now he's nervous about what might happen. "My dad's a doctor. I've been on birth control since I was sixteen. You don't have to worry."

"I'm worried about a lot of things right now." He concentrates on running the wipe along the inside of my thigh. "But getting you pregnant isn't one of them."

He sounds so calm. So sure. The thought of getting me pregnant doesn't even faze him. Like we've been together this whole time. Like it hasn't been five years since I've seen his face anywhere except in my dreams. I can't help but wonder how we got here. What would've happened if he'd stayed.

He throws the wipes away before pulling another handful free. Starting on my other thigh, he concentrates on cleaning himself off me like it's important. The only thing that matters.

"You went into the military." Even though it's not a question, saying it makes me feel weak. I swore I'd never ask. That I didn't care because it didn't matter. *He* didn't matter. He was just a guy. One who lied. Said whatever he had to, to get what he wanted.

But he never made me promises. Never made plans for *later* and he never told me he loved me. Five years later, I need to let that count for something. I need to accept that maybe, just maybe, laying together in the dark, everything Jaxon said to me had been true.

I also need to accept that whether I want to or not, no matter what happens next, I *do* care.

I've always cared.

I don't think he's going to answer me. I think he's kept secrets for so long that he doesn't know how to do anything else.

He finally stops scrubbing and looks up at me, hands resting on my knees, pushing them together. "Do you know what renal agenesis is?"

I nod because I do. "It's a birth defect. It means you were born with only one kidney."

He nods. Seems relieved he doesn't have to explain it. "Simon was born with renal agenesis. In of itself, being born with only one kidney isn't that big of a deal, as long as the one you *do* have is healthy." His fingers dig into my knees slightly. "Simon's wasn't. We were managing it, but then he developed type-one diabetes when he was eight. Within six months, he was on dialysis."

I think about all the times I'd played with him. Chased him through the house. Let him dogpile me in the backyard. Sat him at the kitchen table with a bowl of tomatoes to squish or a bowl of green beans to snap. "I didn't know." My heart lurches in my chest. I've missed him. He wasn't just a kid I babysat for in high school. He was important to me. After Jaxon left, his mother and brother moved away. I never saw them again, and my heart breaks a little whenever I think about it. "Is he okay?"

Please let Simon be okay.

"His medical bills were insane. My mom was working herself to death, trying to keep up with them and watching her try was killing *me*." He shakes his head at me, suddenly angry. Not with me. With himself. "I joined the Marines. That's where I went. They gave me a pretty hefty signing bonus that I used to pay down some of the debt, but the doctors warned me when he was born that Simon was going to need a kidney transplant, sooner or later. Even with an available kidney, that wasn't something I could afford without medical insurance."

I let what he's saying sink in, instantly recognizing that it doesn't make sense.

I'm a pharmacy technician. My dad is a doctor. I understand how medical insurance works. The majority of our conversations revolve around what crooks insurance companies are. Military or not, I know that as his brother, Simon wouldn't be covered by his policy. That's not how insurance works. Siblings aren't covered, but... as soon as it clicks for me, he says it.

"Simon isn't my brother, Claire." The hands on my knees fall away like he's sure that once he says it, I won't want him to touch me anymore. "He's my son."

TWENTY-SEVEN

Jaxon

Simon is my son.

I always imagined telling her. Almost did that night in her room. I almost told her everything.

About how I'd been thirteen when I lost my virginity to a woman more than twice my age. About how my mom, who was working three jobs to support us, asked our next-door neighbor, someone she considered a friend, to keep an eye on me.

About how her idea of keeping an eye on me involved more than helping me with my homework and making sure I ate more than dry cereal for dinner. About how it went on for more than a year before anyone found out.

When the inevitable finally happened, she convinced me to *do the right thing*, which was run away with her. We crossed three state-lines over the course of five days before we were caught. I was fourteen.

She was sentenced to fifteen years in prison—five for every state line she crossed—and Simon was born in a prison hospital ward.

They didn't even tell me. He'd been in a crisis nursery for a week before someone called my mom. If he'd been born healthy, if someone else has wanted him, I have a feeling no one would've bothered.

I was scared shitless. Barely fifteen years old. I didn't even have to shave on a regular basis, and I was a father. I'd never met my own. Didn't know much about him beyond the fact that he didn't want me. Didn't love me.

No matter the circumstances of his birth, there was no way in hell I was going to put my own kid through that. I was going to see this through. Scared or not, I was going to be there.

My mom what devastated. She felt guilty. Like she owned a part of the blame for what happened. No matter how many times I tell her differently, she still thinks she needs forgiveness.

I didn't tell Claire then, but I tell her now. I tell her everything, recognizing that it's something I should've done a long time ago.

She's staring at me, mouth slightly open, and I can see the full spectrum of her emotions on her face. Disbelief. Pity. Disgust. All the things I never wanted to see in her eyes when she looked at me.

Simon is ten, almost eleven. So close to where I was when everything started to happen. If I ever found out that someone had preyed on him like that, I'd kill them. I try not to think about what that means. What that makes me. "I don't consider myself a victim." I shake my head.

Finally out of words, I stop talking. Wait for her to respond. When she doesn't, I run a hand through my hair in frustration. "Say something."

"Where is she now?" She looks blindsided. Like she's having a hard time putting thoughts and words together. "Simon's mother… where is she? Does she—"

"She's in prison." I shoot up from my crouch, angling myself away from her. "Her rights were severed. She doesn't even know where we are."

"Oh..." she nods her head, her face crumpling into a frown like she's trying to process everything I just told her. "Did you love her?"

She doesn't sound angry or jealous. She sounds sad. Sorry for me.

"I thought I did." Jesus. I fucking hate this. Hate talking about it. Hate the way people look at me when they find out. "I was just a dumb kid. I was—"

"You should've told me."

"I know. I'm sorry—" I start to pace, no more than a few strides before I have to turn myself around. "I didn't mean for—"

"You should've *told* me." It comes out more forcefully this time, anger and something else, something I don't want to look at too closely, etched plainly across her face.

"This entire time I thought it was me." She stands, jerking down her skirt before shooting herself into my path. "Something *I* did. Something about *me* that you didn't want, no matter what you said."

Every word is a slap in the face. I have to hold my neck stiff to keep myself from recoiling. My feet planted, so I don't stumble back.

I open my mouth to respond, not sure what's going to come out when I do, but before I can say a word, someone knocks on the door.

Claire reaches over and flings the door open. "What?" she barks loudly. It's her sister. Behind her, the rest of them are huddled together, eyes wide and whispering loudly behind their hands.

Bri jerks back, stunned by her sister's tone. I can tell she's not used to being talked to that way. "I—we..." She looks over her shoulder before refocusing on Claire, looking at her like she's a total stranger. "We're ready to leave."

I look at my watch.

We've been here for nearly an hour.

"Give us a minute," I say, swinging the door closed on Bri's outraged expression. As soon as it's shut, the chatter in the hallway falls silent. They want to hear what I have to say? Fine. I don't give a fuck. I need to finish it. To finally say all the things I should have said to her years ago.

I focus on Claire, her face tipped up so she can glare at me. "I'm sorry," I tell her.

"For which part?" she shoots back, her eyes more green than blue, sharp like glass.

"All of it." I nod, jamming my hands into my pants pockets because I want to grab her. Kiss her. "Everything. I convinced myself that if you knew about Simon—where he came from—you'd think I was..." To blame. I was afraid she'd look at me and think I was at fault somehow. Or worse, feel sorry for me. "I don't know." I free a hand, run it over my face. "I was twenty and the father of a six-year-old. I'm twenty-four. Simon is *ten*. His mother is in *prison*."

"So?" She's looking up at me like nothing I've said matters. Like none of it makes sense, and suddenly, I feel the weight of it. Everything. All of it. I feel it in my bones, and for the first time in a long time, I want to give up.

"So, that's not exactly normal, Claire. I'm not normal. My life isn't normal... nothing about me is." That's the truth. What I should've told her from the very start... but it's not the whole truth. "You deserved better than me, all the way around." I shake my head at her while I reach for the door. "You still do." As soon as I say it, I realize why I avoided telling her the truth for so long. The *real* reason I never told her.

It's because I knew that once I said it out loud, I'd finally get it. That I'd have to stop harboring this ridiculous fantasy of a happily ever after with her. I'd have to admit that Claire St. James is better off without me.

And I'd finally have to let her go.

TWENTY-EIGHT

Claire

Bri's friends are staring at me.

Especially Helena. She looks like she wants to brain me with an empty champagne bottle. They all think I hooked up with some random limo driver in the dressing room of a sex shop. Which is what I did, if you want to get technical about it. If the last thirty minutes have told me anything, it's that I never really knew Jaxon Bennett.

Not even a little bit.

"Claire—"

"It's Jaxon," I tell her because I know what she's going to say. "Jaxon Bennet." Her friends continue to stare at me like I have some sort of contagious disease. For once in my life, I don't give a shit what my sister or her friends think.

When her face remains blank, I shake my head, settling back in the seat. "Are you serious? We went to high school with him, for god's sake."

Her face remains blank. "You told Dad you didn't recognize him."

"Yeah." I roll my eyes before shifting my gaze to stare out the window. "Well, I lied."

We're headed to Grind, the first club on the itinerary where Jaxon's replacement driver will meet us and take over. He's making the arrangements while he drives. I can hear the low murmur of his voice seeping through the privacy partition.

He's leaving again.

I watch the city slip by, splashes of light and shadow hitting the dark tinted glass. Sounds push through the glass. Horns honking. Sirens screeching. Scores of people teem the sidewalks.

Bri and her friends start to chatter, the episode with Jaxon and me fading as their excitement builds. They start freshening their make-up. Fix their hair. Pop another bottle and toast my sister.

"You and Kyle are going to be so happy," Sara gushes, tipping the champagne mag over her empty glass. "You're so lucky."

The rest of them chime in about how amazing the wedding is going to be. How perfect her life is.

I have to press my hand to my mouth to keep myself from laughing out loud. Not because it's funny and not because it's not true.

Because the guy I've been in love with since before I even really knew what love *was*, has a ten-year-old son.

And he left me to save his life.

I can't be mad at him for that, no matter how much I want to be. It's the rest of it I'm having a hard time working my head around.

We pull up in front of Grind and the line to get in is wrapped around the building. I hear Jaxon's door open and shut, watch him circle the car to open the rear door for Bri and her friends. Hand them onto the sidewalk where they cluster together and talk over each other in a loud, excited rush.

His hand appears in the doorway, and I let him help me out of the back of the limo. As soon as I'm on the sidewalk, he lets go of my hand. "Goodbye, Claire." He says it without looking at me.

Not, *I'll see you later*.

Not, *we need to talk about this*.

Not, *give me another chance.*

Goodbye.

This time, Jaxon gives me the closure I need.

And it's the last thing I want.

TWENTY-NINE

Jaxon

When I get home, my mom is dozing on the couch, an open book dangling from her hand and Simon is out cold, sprawled on the floor in front of the television. I stand in the doorway and look at them.

My mother and my son.

It was my mom's idea to pass us off as brothers. She was barely into her 30s when Simon was born, and she wanted me to have a life. A childhood. She didn't want people to look at me and see the fucked-up kid who had a kid of his own, and she wanted Simon to have a chance. I went along with it all because it was easier and because she was right. Not about me but about Simon. He deserved better, more than I could give him.

But I never thought I was ashamed of any of it before Claire. Every time I looked at her, it was all I could think about. What she would think of me if she knew. Not just about Simon, but about the circumstances of his birth. Someone like her would never want someone like me. Not if she knew the truth.

"You're home early."

I look away from Simon to find my mom watching me from the couch.

"Yeah." I nod, tossing my bike keys into the basket by the front door. "I called Thomas. He took over for me." We store our rides in the same garage, and he was willing to grab my bike and meet me at Grind to finish out the job. He met me in front of the club, we exchanged keys, and I left Claire standing on the sidewalk.

At least this time I said goodbye.

"Things went that well, huh?" She gives me a sad smile.

I give her a shrug, looking at Simon. "Did he get his insulin shot?" I say even though it's a ridiculous question.

"Yes, he got his shot." My mom sighs. "Tell me what happened with Claire."

I don't want to talk about it. I know she's going to push the subject, but I try to hold her off as long as I can. "You should probably get home—"

"*Jaxon*."

I sigh, giving up. "I told her," I say, leaning against the doorframe. "I told her everything." As much as it sucks, knowing my suspicions about her potential reaction was well-founded, I'm glad that it's finally over. I'm glad she knows. Maybe now that Claire understands that my leaving had nothing to do with how I felt about her, that there was nothing she did to make it happen, she can move on with her life. I really hope that she can.

Because I can't.

Because now I know she's it for me. There is no moving on. There is no one else.

I'm twenty-four years old, and I'm going to love Claire St. James until the day I die.

"Jax..." My mom sets her book aside and stands, moving toward me so she can wrap me up in her arms like she used to when I was a kid. "I'm sorry."

I hug her back, letting her apologize because it makes her feel better. Setting her away from me, I smile and change the subject. "Did he ask you to stay?"

My mom moved out a couple of months ago, into an apartment a few blocks away. It was my idea. I felt like she needed to have her own place. Start her own life while Simon and I get used to being father and son instead of brothers.

He's known the truth for a while now, why my mom felt like the lie was necessary to give us both a chance at what she calls a *normal life.* He took it surprisingly well. It's the separation from my mother that he's having a hard time with. Why he's so angry at me. He still calls her mom. He still calls me by my first name. I'm not sure we're ever going to get to a place where I'm Dad.

My life is thoroughly fucked up. Claire was right to push me away, and I was right to let her. She deserves more than anything I have to offer. I know that. I *know* that but knowing it didn't stop me from wanting or wishing. Didn't stop me from hoping that maybe I'd get to wake up beside her for once instead of walking away.

"He didn't." She smiles at me, seeing it as progress. "Do you need me to? I can stay if you want to—"

She wants me to go after Claire. I did that once. Let her go, only to chase after her. I was a selfish kid then, too intent on what I wanted to recognize or even care about what was best for her.

Best for us both.

"No." I shake my head, crossing the living room to lift a sleeping Simon into my arms. He's a big kid. Almost as big as I was when I was his age. Even so, feeling the weight of him in my arms, I can clearly remember what it felt like the very first time that I held him. The way his breath puffed against my neck. The way his fingers curled into the collar of my shirt.

"It's not too late." She tries again because all my mother has ever wanted is for me to be happy. "Maybe—"

"Yes, it is. It's been too late for a long time now." I shake my head. "I need to let her go. Let it be over. Move on."

Even as I say it I know it's a lie.

There's not going to be any moving on. Not for me. Because Claire St. James is the one.

The only one.

And I lost her.

THIRTY

Claire

I watch him walk away, and all I can think is, at least this time I'm awake. At least this time I see it coming. At least this time, I *know* Jaxon is leaving me behind.

Running my fingertips across my cheeks, I take a deep breath. Let it out slowly before squaring my shoulders and turning toward my sister and her tight cluster of simpering bridesmaids.

"What are you doing?" Bri says, her finger pointed down the crowded sidewalk. "You're just going to let him get away?"

"Bri—" I'm tired. I'm done. I want to go home.

"Seriously?" She drops her hand, eyes wide. "Go after him. I didn't cancel the limo reservation that we've had for months and steal Dad's credit card to book Jaxon

Bennett at the last minute so I could watch you get your heart broken, all over again."

"You—" I stare at her, not sure I heard her correctly. "You did what? Why? Why would you do that?" Behind her, her friends watch the drama unfold. Tonight's been straight out of a Tele Novella—so insane, it borders on the ridiculous.

Bri reaches for me. Grabbing me by the arm, she shoves me in the direction Jaxon went. "I'll explain later. Right now you need to—"

"No." I plant my feet and shake my head. I'm tired of letting my sister push me around. "You'll explain now."

She rolls her eyes, like what I'm asking for is a waste of time. "A friend of Kyle's booked Jaxon as a driver last weekend and wouldn't stop raving about how great he was—how he could get his clients into VIP and the best tables at any restaurant in Chicago, so I asked for his name to see if I could snag a last minute booking. Sure enough, when I checked the website, there he was."

"I don't understand..." I feel dumb. Like I'm having a hard time putting it all together. "Why?"

"Why?" She looks at me like I'm stupid. "Because I want you to be happy and he's the only—"she stops talking, her shoulders slumping forward for a just a second before standing up straight. "Nope." She shakes her head again. "This isn't happening again." She looks over my shoulder at the driver Jaxon called to replace him. "Do you know where Jaxon lives?" He must've nodded his head because Bri smiles. "Good. Take her there," she says, giving me a hard nudge in his direction.

"Uhhh, no."

I turn around to find a guy, blond hair, dark eyes, wearing a suit very similar to Jaxon's, standing behind me. He shakes his head, splitting a look between me and Bri. "I'm not taking a woman I don't know to my friend's house. That's not happening."

Before I can say a word, Bri advances on him, reaching out to drill a manicured finger into his chest. "You're going to take her," she says, head tipped up to glare at him with narrowed eyes. "Because tomorrow morning, when you take Jaxon his car, you're going to hand him the keys and say, *that crazy bitch wanted me to drive her sister to your house—can't you believe that shit?* And then he's going to know that she tried to come after him and that you wouldn't help her—and *then* he's going to be pissed. At you." She punctuated the last two words with a couple of finger jabs before dropping her hand. "Jaxon Bennett doesn't strike me as someone you want to piss off."

The guy alternates a look between me and Bri, seemingly weighing her words against what he knows about his friend. Finally, he looks at me and sighs.

"Get in."

Twenty minutes later, I'm standing on the front porch of a small, two-story row house in a quiet neighborhood, a lot like the one they used to live in years ago. The tiny front yard is well tended with what looks like a newly planted tree standing sentry over a cobblestone walk, all of it surrounded by an honest-to-god, white picket fence.

I raise my fist to knock but stall out before I can make a sound, letting my hand drop to my side. Suddenly, I don't know what to do. He left me, twice. At what point am I finally going to let him go?

As soon as the thought takes root, I cut it down. My mother left me behind. My sister left me behind. I'm tired of watching people walk away. I deserve more than that... and so does Jaxon.

I know why he left me—then and now. Yes, he left Gailena and joined the military, to make sure Simon would get the medical care that he needs, but he left *me* because he didn't think I'd want him if I knew the truth.

I came to tell him he's wrong. He's wrong now, and he was wrong five years ago. Mind made up, I raise my fist again, coming to within a breath of knocking when the door is pulled open, and I'm face-to-face with Jaxon's mother.

"*Oh*." she jerks back, wide eyes aimed at me for just a second before she goes completely pale. "Claire?" Mrs. Bennett breathes my name softly, and it sounds like a prayer. "*Ohmygod*," she says in a rush before pulling me into her arms. "You're here." Her arms tighten around me for a moment, hands pressed against my back before she pulls away to look at me. "I thought I was going to have to go looking for you..." She pushes me back onto the porch before closing the door behind her. "He said he told you about—" She stops talking. "I know he hurt you, Claire but he was so worried that you wouldn't understand that he convinced himself that you'd reject him. Reject Simon."

"I know." I nod, my hands coming up to grip her arms. "I understand."

And I do understand. But understanding why doesn't make it hurt any less.

She looks at me, her eyes roving over my face before she aims her gaze directly at mine. "Simon still talks about you, he misses you. We all do." She smiles at me. Loosening her grip on me before stepping to the side, she pushes the door open. Even from here I can hear the faint whir of a blender. "He's in the kitchen." She gives me a quick kiss on my cheek before she hurries down the walk.

THIRTY-ONE

Jaxon

I take Simon upstairs and put him to bed, kicking my way through a minefield of Legos and dirty clothes. He is so cleaning his room tomorrow.

I press my lips to his forehead. "Night, buddy." He'll be eleven in three months and if awake, wouldn't let me tuck him in if his life depended on it.

I try to tell myself it's the age and not the fact that things got complicated between us. When I enlisted, I was his big brother. When I came home, I was his father. Trust me, I know how fucked-up it sounds. We're in counseling, and we're working on it. That's all I can do.

"Jax?"

Jax.

He hasn't called me that in a long time. Lately, it's been *Jaxon* or nothing at all. It's not *dad*—I don't know if we'll ever get to a place where he'll feel comfortable calling me dad—but it's a start.

"Yeah?"

"I heard you and Mom talking earlier. About Claire."

Shit.

"Yeah." I clear my throat. Sit back down. "She ended up being the client I drove for tonight."

"Oh." That's all he says but there's more. I can hear it in his tone. Finally, he gives it up. "Did she ask about me?"

"She did." I tell him the truth, or at least a version of it that doesn't make me feel like a total asshole. "She said she misses you."

"Maybe we can go see her." It's not a question. Not really.

"I don't know if that's a good idea."

There's a 50/50 chance she's getting married.

I fucked up.

I left her again.

He gives me a long, measured look. "I'll talk to Mom. She'll take me." He turns onto his side and faces the wall.

"Simon—"

"Night."

Shit.

"Goodnight."

I head to my room, pulling my tie all the way loose as I go. Tossing it and my jacket onto a nearby chair, I strip the rest of the suit off, before pulling on a pair of track pants.

In the kitchen, I mix a quick protein shake—what passes for food when I'm too wiped to cook—adding a couple of frozen bananas and a generous dollop of peanut butter before running it through the blender.

Taking the lid off, I stand at the kitchen sink and drink my dinner. Staring through the window, across the yard, at the small detached garage behind the house, I try to move on.

I've got a couple of loads to wash— Simon's clothes and mine. A load of towels to fold. I'll finish the laundry and wear myself out between loads by working out so hard I won't be able to move tomorrow.

What I *won't* do is think about Claire.

What happened tonight.

How I had my shot and fucked it up, same as before.

Maybe I can still—

I catch a shadow of movement behind me in the reflection of the window, and I turn, expecting to see Simon in the doorway or maybe my mom. But it's not Simon, and it's not my mom.

It's Claire.

She's here.

Standing right in front of me.

I stand here, staring at her, trying to convince myself that this isn't really happening. That I just want her so bad the wanting has finally driven me crazy. I close my eyes and wait for her to go away.

"You really need to stop doing that."

That's when I know it's not a dream. That I haven't finally lost my mind. I know because, in my dreams, the first words out of her mouth are always the same.

I love you.

I open my eyes.

She's still here. I don't know how she found me, but she's *here*, standing in front of me in that barely-there dress and spiked heels that make her legs look like they go on forever. Her hair is loose, falling around her shoulders in gentle waves that make my hands ache, her eyes, more blue than green, staring at me with a mixture of frustration and apprehension.

"Doing what?" I set the pitcher down, leaning against the counter, crossing my arms over my chest.

"Take your pick," she says, closing the distance between us until she's standing right in front of me, close enough to touch, her gaze locked on mine. I remember the first time we stood this close, how nervous she was. How much I wanted to kiss her. She doesn't look nervous now. She looks like she wants to hit me. "Not giving me a say in what happens between us. Disappearing into thin air." She moves, tossing her purse on the table before turning toward me again. "Leaving me behind."

"You don't want me, Claire." I shake my head, tightening the lock I have on my arms, pushing them against my chest to keep myself from reaching for her. "I'm not—"

"We need to be clear about something," she says through her teeth, jabbing me in the chest with her finger. Even with the heels, she has to tip her head back to look me in the eye. "I'm sorry about what happened to you, I am... but it doesn't make a difference to me. It doesn't change the way I feel about you and it doesn't change the way I feel about Simon. What I'm angry about is the fact that you left. You left and didn't trust me enough to even try to tell me why."

"I was trying to protect you." It's a ridiculous thing to say, given the circumstances, and she confirms it when she laughs in my face. "Claire—"

"Shut up, Jaxon," she snaps up at me. "And stop assuming you know how I feel or what I think because you don't. You didn't know then, and you don't know now."

"Okay..." I close my eyes and sigh. "So tell me." My eyes open and I find her where I left her. Close. Too close to allow me to think straight. "What do you want?"

"The same thing I've always wanted," she says softly, her eye gone gray with tears. "You."

THIRTY-TWO

Claire

I don't regret saying it. I probably should, but I don't. He needs to know what he walked away from. What could've been. How things might've happened if only he'd given me a chance.

"And Simon?" I watch his jaw tighten.

"I don't care where Simon came from," I say, feeling like he just slapped me in the face. "I loved him, and you took him *away* from me." The realization tumbles loose, revealing a wound I hadn't realize I'd suffered, the pain of it something I hadn't even let myself consider.

That losing Simon hurt me just as much as losing his father.

"I would've done whatever you asked, Jaxon." I shake my head, force myself to look up at him. His clenched jaw. Tight mouth. Narrowed eyes. The way he won't let himself reach for me. Holds his neck stiff, like every word I'm saying is a slap in the face. He doesn't believe me. Won't let himself.

Still, I have to finish it.

I have to say it, even if it destroys me all over again.

"If you'd said, *come with me, Claire*—I would've. If you'd said, *wait for me*—I would've. If you'd told me that what happened between us was something that would never happen again and that I needed to move on, it would've killed me, but I would've let you go."

"I didn't want to hurt you." He shakes his head. "I—"

"You knew you were going to end up hurting me, either way," I say, talking over him. "You just didn't want to see it."

He doesn't have an answer. Not for that— because it's true. "I was afraid."

His admission stops me cold. "Then tell me now," I say, taking a step back. "What do you want from me? What do *you* want me to do?"

Silence.

Nothing.

He just stares at me, his throat working against things he'll never make himself vulnerable enough to say, but I guess that's my answer, isn't it? Jaxon and I will always be caught somewhere between holding on and letting go.

"You can't say it, can you?" I shake my head. "You're still afraid. I'm standing here, right in front of you, begging you to let me in, and you still can't believe…" I catch my breath. Let it out on a sigh. "Okay." I turn around, picking my purse up off the table. I'm crying now, my shoulders trembling with the effort to hold it all in. "Goodbye, Jaxon."

I leave. Through the kitchen doorway and down the hall, the way I'd come, on legs so numb I feel like I'm floating.

Reaching for the front door, my arm hanging in front of me like a ghost, I pull it open. I don't know where I'm going. I don't know how I'm going to get there, but I'm the one who's leaving this time. I'm not going to be left behind again.

From the corner of my eye, I see a large hand shoot past me to slap against the door, snapping it closed in front of my face, the bulk of him looming over me.

"Stay."

He says it softly, the breath of it falling across my bare shoulder, his free hand sliding along in its wake, brushing my hair over it to move down my back. "That's what I want." I feel his lips against the back of my neck, a soft, languid press that leaves me reeling. "I want you to stay."

I feel my breath catch in my throat as his hand slides into my hair. His fingers tightening, he turns my head, angling up, my chin tipped over my shoulder. "Will you..." He skims his lips across my wet cheeks, his hand falling away from the door to turn me toward him. His mouth hovers over mine, his gaze locked on my face. "Will you stay with me? With us?"

I nod, pulling his face to mine with a smile as I whisper the word I've been waiting five years to say to him.

"Yes."

THIRTY-THREE

Jaxon

I can't get her upstairs fast enough.

Truthfully, I'm not even sure how I managed it. All I know is she said yes.

I asked Claire to stay and she said yes.

Yes.

After that, everything was a blur.

I must've picked her up because I'm holding her. I must've carried her upstairs because we're in my room, the dim light from my bedside lamp shining softly, standing at the foot of my bed.

I turn, setting her on her feet to stand in front of me before I sink down, sitting on the edge of the bed. Enthralled, I watch her reach down, taking off one shoe and then the other before dropping them on the floor.

"No," she says softly, her hands reaching for the small of her back so she can work down the zipper of her dress.

"No?" I can feel my brow furrow, worried about what she's about to say, even while I can't look away from the sight of her undressing in front of me.

"No," she says, a slight smile playing at the corners of her mouth as she works her hips to shimmy out of the tight, black dress she's wrapped in. Baring her breasts. Her soft belly. The whisper of lace between her thighs. "I'm not getting married."

Unable to take another second of not touching her, I nod, even as I'm reaching for her. "That's good," I tell her as I close a trembling hand over her breast, giving it a gentle squeeze as I lift it to my mouth. "I was wondering if I was going to have to kill someone." I look up at her and she pushes he hands through my hair with a gasp when I draw her nipple into my mouth to give it hard, greedy pulls that tighten it instantly against my tongue.

"Don't you mean worrying?" she says, her voice thin and soft.

I snake an arm around her waist, pulling her closer, turning and falling until I have her under me, stretched out across the bed.

Even as I move her, I can't take my mouth off her. My fingers digging into the soft, yielding flesh of her hip while I devour her, my tongue licking its way over feverish skin. Between her breasts. Across her belly to dip into her navel. The place where her leg meets her hip. Trailing slowly along the inside of her thigh until I'm there. Right where I need to be.

"No, I mean *wondering,* because there's no use worrying about something I can't change," I tell her grazing her tender pink flesh with my teeth. "I'd kill any other man who tried to claim you."

"Jax—" The rest of my name gets snagged on a sharp, ragged gasp when I drag my tongue up the center of her and she sighs, her hands cradling the back of my head, even as she's lifting her hips to press herself against my mouth, rubbing herself against my tongue.

"Still greedy," I growl against her, nipping and sucking at her with my lips and teeth, slipping my hands under her ass to lift her, pressing her pussy against my face so I can fuck her with my tongue.

"*Yes…*" she moans softly, her hips rocking in my hands, my shoulders pushing against her thighs, opening her even further so I can taste every part of her I've been missing.

Needing.

"Jesus Christ, Claire." My breathing is harsh and shallow, every push and draw of my lungs against her like torture to us both. "As warm and sweet as I remember," I say, circling her swollen clit with the tip of my tongue.

Closing my mouth over the top of her, I slip a finger inside, long and slow, and start to suck her off, matching each stroke I'm giving her to the pulls of my mouth until she's writhing and bucking on the bed underneath me, her soft cries and grasping hands pushing me so close the edge, I'm about to come from just the feel of her against my tongue. The taste of her in my mouth. Her hands in my hair.

She lets out a sharp, shuddering gasp and her thighs slam closed around my head even as her pussy locks around my finger, each pulsing clench of it trying to draw me deeper. Keep me inside her.

I let out a groan of my own, suddenly so eager to get my cock inside her that I'm shaking. Strung out. It doesn't matter that I was buried inside her only a few hours ago. It doesn't matter that we have a lifetime together. That I asked her to stay with me and she said yes. I need to fuck her so bad I can feel my bones cracking under the weight of it.

I lever myself up and over her enough to yank my pants down around my hips before settling between her parted thighs, the head of my throbbing cock pressed against her.

"Wait," she pants out, eyes wide. Small hand pressed against my shoulder.

Shit. Right. "I don't have a condom." I squeeze my eyes shut and let out a long breath, instantly backing off. "It's been a while since I—"

"That's not why I stopped you."

My eyes pop open and I look down to see her staring up at me, her hand still pressed against my shoulder. "Did I hurt you?" I feel my face fall into a scowl. "Did I do something to—"

"No..." The hand on my shoulder slips down, skimming down my pec, fingers bumping along the tight muscles in my abdomen. "It's my turn," she says, her lids lowering over blueish gray eyes as her hand wraps around my cock. "I want to know if you taste as good as I remember."

Holy shit.

My eyes slam shut again and I groan. Push myself into her grip, pumping my hips against her hand. "Claire..." I growl her name, the muscles at the base of my spine tightening so hard and fast, it almost hurts. "I'm struggling here."

She lets go of me to throw her leg over my hip and turns, pushing me flat on the mattress to straddle my stomach. "Then relax," she says, bending over me to press her mouth to my throat. "And let me do what I want."

"What's that?" I groan softly because I want to hear her say it. I like the blush that spills across her cheeks when she talks dirty.

"I want your cock in my mouth," she whispers in my ear before licking her way down the taut cords of my neck. My collarbone. My pecs. Abs. Teeth scraping against my hipbone. My dick jerking every time her a part of her brushes against the base of my shaft. Pre-cum leaking from the tip at a steady pace, faster and faster the closer her mouth gets to where she's going.

If she keeps it up, we're not going to get that far.

She goes still. Stops touching me. Stops teasing me and somehow that's worse.

"Claire?" I crunch upward, drawing my elbows up and underneath me so I can look down at her. She's looking at my scar. Raised and pink over the place where one of my kidneys used to be. The one I gave to my son.

The reason I left her all those years ago.

I open my mouth to say something.

Claire.

I'm sorry.

I love you.

If you'll let me, I'll spend the next seventy years making it up to you. Every day, for the rest of our lives.

Whatever it is, she doesn't give me the chance.

She leans in, pressing her lips to the scar, kissing it so reverently, it feels like worship.

It feels like forever.

THIRTY-FOUR

Jaxon

I knew, even before I opened my eyes.

Claire is gone.

I lay there for a while, eyes closed, thinking about the night before.

Stay.

I'd finally said it. Finally told her what I wanted. I told her the truth, I told her everything and she stayed with me. Let me take her upstairs. Get her naked. Take her to bed.

We talked for hours. Kissed and laughed. I held her until my lids grew heavy and I followed her into sleep.

I love you.

That was the last thing I said to her before I dropped off.

I love you too.

That's what she said.

Then she left.

And it's no less than I deserve.

I hear noises coming from downstairs. The refrigerator opening and closing. The slide of silverware in the drawer. Someone rifling around in the pantry.

Simon.

I've tried to make Sunday breakfast a thing but he sabotages me, every chance he gets. If I'm not up, making pancakes before he comes downstairs, he slams a quick bowl of cereal so he can tell me he's already eaten.

I guess I deserve that too.

Swinging my legs over the side of the bed, I sit on its edge and stare out the window while the pressure in my chest crushes the air from my lungs.

You know what? Fuck that.

Yes, I've made mistakes, but I was a kid. A kid who was a father. Scared shitless, just trying to keep my head above water. Yes, I could've done better but I tried.

I'm *still* trying.

I stand, stalking my way across the room. Pulling a pair of jeans from my drawer, I jerk them up, barely closing the zipper before finding a T-shirt. Jam my feet into boots without socks.

Claire said she was going to stay.

I told her what I want and she said yes.

If she changed her mind, I deserve to know why.

Even if I don't deserve it, she's going to look me in the eye and tell me anyway.

And if I don't like the answer…

I take the back stairs into the kitchen where Simon is. I'll call my mom. She'll come over and stay with him. I'll take my bike. Fuck, I'll walk if I have to.

I'm going to get her.

I'm bringing her home.

Because, Simon and I—we're her home.

"Hey, Simon, I—"

I stop short, what I'm seeing in front of me rooting me in place.

Claire.

She's standing at the stove, her back to me, swimming in a pair of my pajama pants and an old T-shirt from my drawer. Simon's at the kitchen table, making his way through a stack of pancakes.

When I speak, Simon looks up from his plate and Claire turns around, both of them looking right at me.

"Where are you going?" Claire says, her brow scrunched.

"I'm going to find you." I probably look like I feel. Disheveled. Insane.

Her lips twitch. "Do you have time for breakfast before you leave?"

I rush her, crossing the kitchen in a few long strides to pull her into my arms. Lifting her off the ground, I crush her against me. "You're here," I say against her neck, breathing in the smell of her.

"I am." She laughs, pulling back just enough to see my face. "Where else would I be?"

Nowhere.

Because this is where she belongs.

Where she's always belonged.

"Hey, Simon—" I lift my face and turn to find him watching us. "Should we ask Claire to stay?"

"For dinner?" he says, a goofy grin plastered all over his face. He has questions, I'm sure, but he looks happy. Happier than I've seen him in a long time. For the first time since I've been home, I don't just hope. I *know* we're going to be okay.

I look down at her and smile. Taking her face in my hands, I smooth my thumbs over her cheekbones, reveling in the feel of her soft skin. The color of her eyes, a soft, muted blue, aimed up at me. I lean down, lowering my mouth to brush it against hers and she sighs, the breath of it skimming across my lips as hers stretch into a smile to match my own. "Dinner could work," I say without looking away from her. "But I was thinking more along the lines of forever."

The End

Want to read about Claire's sister, Bri? You can find her story in GRIND, volume 2 of my One Night series by Ardor Press.

About the Author

Megyn Ward lives on coffee, chocolate and more than the occasional glass of red wine. When she's not spending time with the people who live inside her head, she's raising her four kids under the relentless Arizona sun and praying for a rainy day.

You can connect with her on Facebook or check out her website megynward.com.